Shaletha

Romance in Manhattan

Louis Alexandre Forestier

Published in 2016 in the USA

This is a work of fiction. Names, characters, businesses, places, events and incidents are either the products of the author's imagination or used in a fictitious manner. Any resemblance to actual persons, living or dead, or actual events is purely coincidental.

CAST OF CHARACTERS

SHALETHA MOORE: AFRICAN American fashion designer born in Harlem.

Helen and Ezra Moore: Shaletha´s parents.

Alyssa Moore: Shaletha´s younger sister.

Zion Moore: Shaletha´s problematic brother.

Jacob Moore: Ezra´s brother. Former policeman

Adrian Bianchi: Young Argentine illegal immigrant.

Arionna Jackson: Lawyer. Shaletha´s closest friend.

Kevin Driscoll: Arionna´s husband. History professor.

Ivan Stasevich: Young Russian student. Alyssa Moore´s boyfriend.

Yuri Stasevich Ivan´s father.

John Lewis: Pastor of the Helen and Ezra Moore.

Congregation.

Thomas Williams: Police officer, an old friend of Ezra.

Sebastian, Teresa and Federico Bianchi: Adrian´s parents and brother.

CHAPTER 1

WHEN SHE ENTERED THE room that had been hers when she was a girl the woman felt a knot in her stomach. This happened every time she visited her parents´ house and checked the state of her old belongings. All dolls and stuffed toys were perfectly aligned on her old bed as had been the last time she had entered the room and as they had never been when she occupied it. Some of the posters glued or nailed to the walls with her musical idols of yesteryear still miraculously remained in place, leaving some lighter boxes on the wall where had been those who had fallen.

The woman ran a hand affectionately on the fully armed bed and memory evoked a thousand remembrances of her happy childhood and adolescence. She was then startled by her mother's voice calling her from the ground floor.

"¿Shaletha. Are you okay?"

Immediately after she heard of her father´s deep voice scolding his wife.

"Helen, Shaletha is in her room; leave her alone with her memories."

Shaletha removed with her fingertips a tear peeking from her right eye, composed her throat and answered.

"I´ll be right down Mom."

On leaving she looked in the mirror placed in her wardrobe, which would certainly be filled with the clothes she had left behind when she moved. Shaletha then took a long look to her front and behind with a critical eye and then moaned with satisfaction approving the image that the mirror reflected. Her silhouette was a perfect example of a black woman, with well marked feminine attributes, which since high school provoked comments of her fellow students of all races, particularly those Italians. What the mirror showed her was a firm bust, generous hips, round thighs, well shapely legs and a rear that had always caused envy of her classmates, especially the white girls. The face, certainly beautiful, was framed by a discreet hairstyle away from the fashion of African braids and dreadlocks.

"Shaletha, what is what you need? What is missing to you? The woman sighed without knowing exactly what she meant. She locked the room and went downstairs to talk to her parents.

The dinner conversation had turned almost exclusively on Shaletha´s life. The mother insisted in asking questions about her love life on which she did not have much to tell, and this concerned Helen, while her father asked her affectionately about her working life, a much more satisfying theme for both.

After a silence Helen began to complain about Alyssa´s behavior, the youngest daughter of the Moore family.

"She´s already nineteen, and now is flirting with those white boys, who we already know what are expecting from her." Said plaintively Helen.

"You should not complain woman." Answered angrily the father. "Alyssa has always steered clear of drugs and alcohol. Her grades in school are more than acceptable and we expect she will be able to attend college. She has never brought us problems as his brother has."

The words were followed by silence. Zion, the second son of the Moore family had recently been released from prison and was fulfilling a plan of rehabilitation for his addiction to drugs. Helen groaned and burst into tears.

"Dad that was a low blow." Replied Shaletha. "You know Zion is an open wound for Mom."

The man obviously regretted his words, rose from his chair and ran to hug his wife. The reaction served Shaletha to revalue again the values of the home in which she had grown up. The woman walked over and hugged her parents while she also wiped a tear. The tender scene lasted even a moment until Helen's breathing regularized.

"Why do you take Alyssa's friends to heart?" Asked Shaletha to her mother. "Have you got reasons to think they are bad companies?"

"We have no way to know." Said the father. "We have never met them or talked to them."

" The problem is that in this way we are destroying the foundations of the black family." Helen replied.

"Mom. It is not fair to blame Alyssa for destiny of the black family in this country. She has enough responsibility at her age trying to be happy."

Before it got dark Shaletha decided to undertake the journey back home. She said goodbye to her parents and left their house heading for the nearest subway station. She recalled her childhood in that area of Harlem, when the inhabitants lived confined to their homes and did not venture to remain in the streets after the first shadows fell. When walking Shaletha saw a movement among the shadows in a corner where there was no lighting, no doubt a young couple warmly embracing ignoring the environment surrounding them. Shaletha had necessarily passed by them on her way without the kids perceiving her presence. As she discreetly looked at them her heart sank. At the dim light she could see the blond hair of the young boy mixed with the dark skin of the girl. As she recognized the faces Shaletha did not know for a moment how to react. Alyssa was passionately kissing who a few days earlier had presented as a simple college classmate, a Russian born named Ivan with a last name impossible to remember.

The woman took the subway at the 125th Street station and at that late time managed to travel sitting. In the long journey her mind connected the recent events with certain thoughts that lately recurrently returned to her mind. At thirty-three years Shaletha Moore could not complain about her life or her achievements. After her studies she had found work as a fashion designer at a major textile firm. Important business involving a lot of money depended on her decisions and she was well paid for her work. She had moved from Harlem and had finally rented a totally renovated and very well equipped old apartment in Brooklyn Heights, a quiet and well connected area located just minutes away from their work. When taking vacations Shaletha could afford to choose the best beaches around the continent, which were her favorite destinations. For work reasons she was constantly traveling throughout the Americas and Europe. She was always elegantly dressed and could allow every whim, which anyway were very discreet. She spoke well and was invited to all kinds of events, in which her profession was lavish. They were not little achievements for a girl from Harlem. And yet ...

From some cell phone or a tablet arose amid the noise of the subway running at full speed the notes of an old interpretation of The Rose by Bette Midler.

When the night has been very lonely
And the road has been too long
And you think that love is only
For the lucky and the strong ...

CHAPTER 2

THE FOLLOWING WEEKEND Shaletha decided to attend after a very long time the Sunday morning service at the Baptist Church in Harlem where she used to go as a child. The delighted pastor received her at the church door along with the rest of the parishioners and the woman sat roughly where she used to sit in her infancy.

Contact with the old seats and the peculiar smell of the temple evoked all kinds of memories that finally made her spring a sigh. Of those at sight she only recognized some vaguely familiar faces, and noticed there was a large presence of children. All members of the congregation were African-Americans with different skin tones. Shaletha was not planning to pass that Sunday by her parents' house because she wanted to clarify her ideas and reflect in solitude; that was why she had chosen a service at a different hour than that at which Ezra and Helen usually concurred.

The preaching was in charge of a new pastor and his theme was basically the fight against drugs and the support to the maintenance of the traditional black family against all new and old dangers that lurked in the big city. The woman mused that after twenty years the subjects were basically the same as those of her early adolescence, despite the obvious changes that had occurred in Harlem. She left the church after the end of worship and while the magnificent choir sang their traditional songs. Shaletha felt that the sermon, that years before would have caused her satisfaction and peace of mind, was however opposing some process that was happening inside her and that the woman could not define. She left the church with certain uneasiness.

Shaletha took the subway to go to Brooklyn Heights and again during the whole journey a fight that she could not understand developed within her, a restlessness which she could not escape.

When the subway reached her destination she looked at the watch and realized that it was already noon. As there was little food in her fridge and she did not feel like cooking Shaletha decided to enter a coffee shop where she used to lunch on weekends. She sat at an empty table and waited for the waitress to come over. Idly watching the mirrors surrounding the local the woman secretly saw what her eyes were looking for. He was three tables away, and sat facing her so that against her desires she could observe him at will. Very young, white skin, red hair and light eyes, dressed very simply with a plaid shirt and a sweater tied around his neck, he was finishing his lunch. Although he was obviously sitting, Shaletha could see that he was tall and thin. The woman had already glimpsed him a few times in that location at the same time and had to admit to herself that the decision to go to lunch that Sunday had been in part motivated by the desire to see him again.

Suddenly the boy lifted his eyes that met those of Shaletha, who immediately blushed and taken by surprise looked elsewhere for a moment, but then an inner drive forced her to stare at him; the fact that the young man held her gaze gave Shaletha an inner joy, as if she had achieved a small victory. In fact she had confirmed that also he was really interested. At that time the waitress came with the dish requested.

Shaletha finished eating and got up to go to the ladies room. In the mirror she found that the boy's eyes followed her. The woman unconsciously began to walk swinging significantly her hips. Shaletha was well aware that her buttocks would move provocatively and wanted to control her pace but eventually some wild drive inside her prevailed.

"To hell." Shaletha said to herself while the mirror confirmed to her that his gaze was fixed on her butt.

Going into the bathroom she backed herself on a wall and said aloud.

"But what are you doing? I've never behaved like that in my life!" But another part of her consciousness answered. "And that's why you feel the way you feel. Do what you have to do to get what you want!"

After debating with her for a moment and feeling silly for it Shaletha came out of the ladies room and returned to the hall. Her stomach squeezed as she saw the boy's table empty. One half of her heart told her.

"You surrender now? He did not even wait for your return."

Somewhat ruefully the woman returned to her table and called the waitress asking for the bill. As she received the banking card the waitress pointed to a small paper folded in half and placed on the table that Shaletha had failed to see.

" Lady, does this belong to you?"

Shaletha opened the paper, and her heart skipped a beat with joy as she read the contents.

"I'll wait for your call

Swirl

Adrian"

And below the text there was a phone number.

CHAPTER 3

SHALETHA HAD NEVER been so confused in her life. She had had several casual relationships with men before, even with some white ones, but they were ephemeral ties rarely exceeding two nights, and had never been seriously considered. What she was going through now was uncharted territory, so she decided to do what she did in those rare cases, discuss the issue with her friend and confidant Arionna Jackson, the only person with whom Shaletha allowed herself to share intimate subjects.

Arionna was also African American, born in Texas and was thirty-seven years. She exercised her profession in the Bronx as a lawyer specialized in family issues and human rights. She was a very intelligent, well informed woman and that's why her opinion was taken seriously into account by Shaletha. An additional reason to seek her advice was that she had married a couple of years earlier Kevin Driscoll, a History professor of Irish origin with whom Arionna was deeply enamored. In Shaletha's reasoning this situation guaranteed a quick understanding of the issue that concerned her because Arionna would have been in the same situation some time before.

They had met years earlier when Shaletha moved to Brooklyn Heights and was somewhat lost in the new environment, with few black people around after living all her previous life in Harlem. Shaletha considered that the decision to leave her parents' house had been correct and represented a big step forward in her maturation process.

Shaletha had ringed Arionna the day before and had learnt that Kevin had traveled to give lectures in California, which assured the women the opportunity to speak with absolute freedom. Although Shaletha had not told her friend what subject she wanted to talk about Arionna realized that there was some confusion in her close friend's head.

Shaletha pressed the doorbell and within seconds the door opened. Arionna was still wearing her professional attire because she had just arrived from her studio. She was a dark-skinned woman, slightly overweight and with a cheerful face, with prominent buttocks which she jokingly commented were what had seduced her husband Kevin. As she saw Shaletha appearing at her door with a half-full bottle of whiskey in her hand the hostess said in a festive mood.

"Well, this must be something serious."

After Shaletha's confusing explanation her friend spent a moment meditating in search of the tip of the iceberg.

"Listen, from what I understand you've reached a point in your life in which you've decided you need to put a man into it."

Somewhat surprised by the way of exposing the problem, Shaletha had yet to admit that it was a crude but fair description.

"That does not surprise me at all." Went on Arionna." In fact I think it should have happened long ago, and I clearly told so you repeated times. But of course this is your maturation process and what matters are your own times and not my opinion."

Shaletha returned to serve whiskey, and both had the perception that they would end up getting moderately drunk, but it did not matter because it was a Friday evening.

"I find amazing what you told me about the show that you gave to that young man in the cafeteria, because I cannot imagine you shaking your hips to seduce a man, let alone in a public place. Yet I assure you that if the boy noticed you it was not for your show but for your extraordinary beauty."

"You make me blush again."

"I am just saying the truth. Now ..." Arionna handled the subject with a total professionalism, as if she was in front of a customer at her attorney office. "What I fail to understand is what the reason for your conflict is. You have found a man you like, although you do not want to admit it, and apparently he also likes you, surely for the reason I said before."

The woman stared at her friend in an interrogative way, but Shaletha had no answer to give.

"So I have the right to assume that the reason of what I called "your conflict" is because he is white and somewhat younger than you. I'm right?"

At these words Shaletha had a slight tremor of psychic origin; her friend had hit the mark and had expressed something she knew but did not want to recognize.

"Then... "Continued hypothesizing Arionna. "You've said to yourself, let's talk with my friend Arionna who must have gone through the same process before me."

Shaletha nodded. She congratulated herself for having turned to her friend, who had caught and expressed so clearly an issue that she had trouble recognizing and accepting.

"Well..." Went on Arionna. "In this you are completely wrong." She smiled at Shaletha's gesture of surprise. "Not for a moment the fact that Kevin is white worried me at all. Actually I have to confess that I always liked white boys and dated them in my time at the University. I never paid attention to all these racial cobwebs that make you feel a traitor by looking for a man with another skin color. Really they are just reverse racism, which only seek to turn human beings apart but with other criteria. The first reason to choose a man is that you like him. For the improvement of the species is the woman who must be selective, since the male is seduced and dragged by the weapons every woman should know how to handle. You have all the resources to your advantage to seduce any black, white or green man, you can choose whoever you want."

Arionna sipped the rest of her whiskey so that her friend filled the glasses again.

"You must take charge of your potential, that in the selection of your man is huge and set aside all the nonsense they put inside your head in your family, in Harlem and in your church. All these fabrications serve the purpose of ensuring that black women remain as a huge hunting ground for black men without any other choice. If you want to be at peace with your conscience you can come to the church where I go every so often, not only accepting of interracial relationships, but also homosexual couples."

As the bottle of Scotch was already coming to an end Arionna asked.

"'Well, you do you specifically know about him?'"

Shaletha reached into her purse and pulled out the folded paper found in the coffee shop, then handed it to her friend.

"¿Adrian? Is he American?"

"I do not know."

"You do not know? You have not called him yet?"

"No. I was waiting to meet you before calling."

"You are crazy! You find the man you want, you shake your buttocks to seduce him, he leaves a message and you don't call him? Woman. You have to hammer on hot steel. He will believe that you are not interested or will you find another black or white ass wiggling in front of him."

"If so, let him find it and leave me alone!"

"No! You' can't be saying that seriously. Tonight we're very drunk, but you call him tomorrow morning in front of me. You promise?"

"I promise. Tell me one more thing. What does this word Swirl mean to you? The truth is that I find it intriguing."

"It's the name of a grassroots organization that seeks to help communities of mixed blood to honor their heritage. They are here in New York and elsewhere. But I know it is used in a narrower sense."

"What sense?"

" White boys who want to date black girls and black girls who want to date white boys often use it."

"And what do you think it means in this piece of paper?"

" At least that this Adrian wants to sleep with you and at best that he wants to ensure that you will wiggle your ass just for him in the future."

" I wonder whether this is flattering or arrogant." Shaletha mused.

"Think carefully before giving any exclusivity."

"You're talking about my ass."

"Exactly."

They took the last sip. Shaletha suddenly asked.

"Tell me. How is it living with a white man? I mean sexual life." Shaletha could not believe she had asked that.

"As I recall, you've had some experience yourself."

"Those were isolated incidents. What is the day to day experience?

"The day to day is ... every other day."

"Really? Is that sustainable?"

"With a Viagra every now and then. If Kevin can ′t sustain it, I will seek one who can."

As Shaletha′s face reflected alarm her friend burst out laughing managing to calm her down.

"We are keeping this rhythm because we want to have a baby this year in order to meet our long term plan."

"What plan is that?"

"We want to have at least three children while we are still young."

"Is that the plan of both of you or just yours?"

"In these things the woman has a decisive role."

"It's the plan of a black woman."

"The fact that I have married a white boy does not change my race."

"Well, it's two in the morning. I think I'll go home now."

"No way. You are not able to walk three blocks alone, let alone at night. You stay here."

"But you have only one bed."

"We'll share it. When Kevin is not here I feel cold at night. I hope you will not dream that you are sleeping with Adrian and you get romantic with me ... although on a second thought, maybe it would be an experience."

Seeing the alarm in her friend's face Arionna laughed loudly again.

"You're too easy to scandalize. You have no idea the kind of things I have to hear every day in my profession. Come on, I'll leave the first turn in the bathroom to you."

CHAPTER 4

THE PHONE RANG THREE times, after which a male voice answered. Shaletha had a moment of hesitation, but she looked at Arionna who was urging her with her gestures.

"¿Adrian? My name is Shaletha. I am the woman you saw in the coffee shop."

"The beautiful girl I saw in the coffee shop." Corrected the man.

"Well, at least you know who you are talking to."

"There are not many women in this city who have my phone number." His voice exuded calm, which was just what Shaletha needed.

"You call New York "this city". Where are you from?"

"From Buenos Aires."

"From Buenos Aires, Argentina?

"Yes".

"And do you live in New York permanently?"

"I'll tell you when we meet."

Shaletha was afraid to show anxiety in her interrogation. Once she was convinced that the conversation was going on fluently Arionna rose from the couch and went to the kitchen to prepare breakfast. She had insisted that as soon as they woke up the following day her friend called the man before going home, so as to ensure that the contact was not postponed.

Soon Shaletha came into the kitchen. She looked radiant.

"Well. What news have you got?"

"We'll meet today at seven in the afternoon." Cried joyful Shaletha.

"Going out on a Saturday night, not bad for a start."

Shaletha hugged her friend.

"You know, I'm so glad for having confided this to you."

"You did the right thing. If I had not pushed you you'd still be floating around helplessly. I cannot believe that at your age you are still so hesitant about your relationships. Now go home. Kevin just called me and told me he is on the way from the airport. I have to fix the bed so he will not suspect I have been slept with a man."

"Kevin would never think that."

"It is true. The truth is that we must regain the sex rhythm as soon as he arrives. So today I'll have sex before you and with greater certainty."

"He's surely coming back home tired."

"His problem. Good luck this evening with your white boy Ariel."

"Adrian."

"Whatever."

Shaletha was gathering her things. Arionna appeared suddenly and slapping her forehead said.

"One last thing. Before giving you what he wants demand him to perform oral sex to you. You have to adopt it as common practice."

Shaletha felt her blushed out of embarrassment.

"But I never ..."

"Exactly as I supposed. Make sure it becomes a practice from the beginning. A beautiful girl like you has the right to demand it."

"I do not know how ..."

"You'll find a way. Sunday morning I want a detailed report of how things went."

"But Kevin will be home tomorrow."

"I will send him to the Promenade to walk the dog."

"You have no dog."

"I'll think of something."

Shaletha went back home. She made a brief overview of what happened in the last two days and once again congratulated her for having gone to talk to her friend. Arionna had a strong character and could shake her friend´s head when was needed; "Shake the birdcage." on her own terms. Not only was Shaletha happy for having achieved an appointment but felt liberated, freed from a host of obstacles and impediments for his life. These hurdles had been inculcated at home long before along with so many good principles, and it was time to separate the wheat straw.

Shaletha entered the coffee shop and immediately all eyes turned to her, the men with admiration and women, particularly the white ones, with envy. She saw him sitting in the back watching her with his mouth open. She walked to his table and he rose in a gentle gesture. He took her hand and said.

"You're dazzling... In my country, we kiss women on the cheek. Will you let me?"

"Even those you do not know?"

"Yes. It is not considered abusive. Can I do it with you?"

In response Shaletha placed her cheek and the man planted a chaste kiss. He pulled out a chair for her to sit, and only sat once she had done before."

"I see you in Buenos Aires keep manners."

"Regrettably not all do. But yes, I think that compared to New York you could say that."

"Tell me who you are, what is your job ... well, you know, introduce yourself."

"Well, I'm Adrian Bianchi, and I was not actually born in Buenos Aires but in a small village in the Province of Santa Fe called Hughes, where my parents own a plot of agricultural land as most people in the area. You would call them farmers. I moved to Buenos Aires to study at the University."

"What have you learned?"

"Industrial design."

"How long have you been in New York?"

"About six months."

"You speak very good English. Your accent is unknown to me, it does not sound like Latin."

"We have our own accent, even in Spanish."

"How did you say your last name is?"

"Bianchi."

"It sounds Italian."

"It is."

"You do not look Italian."

"My grandparents came from Northern Italy, the regions called Lombardy and Piedmont, as most people living in our village."

"And the Lombards are blond and blue-eyed?

"Sometimes".

Shaletha felt very at ease with the course the talk had taken. She approached the boy and said in a sweet tone.

"Your eyes are green, not blue as I thought. One more question. What are you doing in New York?"

"I have a job at a newspaper in the Spanish Harlem. It's an ... illegal job. I have a tourist visa and it is expiring." The man looked uneasy for the first time.

"I see. And what do you do there?"

"Graphic design."

"It's not your specialty".

"No, but I have enough knowledge, I do well."

"How old are you?"

"Twenty-four."

The answer, although expected intimately pleased Shaletha. Having a date with a handsome and young man filled her with pleasure along with some felling of guilt.

"Your turn." He said.

"My turn to do what?"

"Of telling me about you."

" Well, I'm Shaletha Moore, born in Harlem, a few blocks away from the 125th street. I have graduated as a fashion designer and work in my profession."

"It looks you are doing well."

"I cannot complain. Ah! I am thirty three years old."

The boy did not make any comments; he looked instead at her with a smile and put his hand over hers.

"Shaletha. You're a very beautiful woman."

"You mean very beautiful for a black woman."

"Nooo! I mean spectacularly beautiful."

The compliment although expected and even provoked, pleased Shaletha especially because it was coming from that boy.

The conversation turned to other subjects, including sports and recreational activities. Adrian finally asked.

"What's your idea for a Saturday night?"

"What do you mean?"

"Where would you like to go?"

"Maybe dancing. How about it?"

"Well, although I'm an awful dancer."

"We can think of something else, I do not want you to feel uncomfortable."

"Are you a good dancer?

"You probably know that we blacks have a natural flair for dancing."

"Then you can teach me."

The upbeat music had been replaced by slow melodies. Adrian took Shaletha by the waist and approached both bodies. As the man was quite higher than she he bowed his head until their foreheads touched. The breasts of the woman rested on his chest. Adrian turned his head a little and approached his lips to Shaletha 's mouth. She opened her lips.

The kiss was long and turned progressively ardent. The man introduced his tongue in her mouth and pulled it out.

"You've very beautiful lips."

"Also a feature of my race."

The tongues joined again whilst Adrian left hand rested on the woman´s buttocks which he began to caress.

"You do not lose time." Whispered Shaletha.

"You want me to pull out my hand?

"Not really." She answered blushing. "Anyway the place is dark."

"You want to stay here or do something else?"

Shaletha growled annoyed with herself. As she was really interested in the man and thought he was interested in her she had made up her mind not go to bed on the first date but now the hormones of both were boiling.

"Where do you live?" She asked the boy.

"In Flushing, Queens."

"Is too far. Do you want to come to my place? It is very close to the coffee shop where we met."

CHAPTER 5

AS SOON AS THEY TRANSPOSED the apartment door the instincts repressed overnight broke loose in a landslide. Adrian pressed Shaletha against the wall close to the door and both joined in a passionate kiss and hug. His hands lifted her skirt which she had carefully dressed and stroked her thighs and buttocks. Shaletha unbuttoned his shirt and kissed his chest covered by reddish hair. Adrian took the woman in his arms as Shaletha showed him the direction of the bedroom. Once there the man threw her on the bed with a certain roughness, lifted her dress and pulled her panties. Without saying a word he introduced his face in her genitals and performed oral sex until she began to moan as she rocked her hips while riding his face. When it was obvious that the woman was highly excited Adrian pulled his pants down and amid convulsions introduced himself deeply into her sex until both reached a synchronous orgasm. Once the frenzy was over Adrian dropped his weight on her and both remained exhausted, sweaty and motionless.

The unions repeated several times separated by brief periods, and finally the young man toured her body with his hands and lips producing an enhanced pleasure to Shaletha by the sense of peace and fulfillment achieved once her anxieties were calmed.

Shaletha watched his bedfellow and wondered if he was asleep; as alerted by a hidden sense he opened one eye and smiled. The woman felt like talking, but knew she could not restart the interrogation she had carried on at the beginning in order not upset the man. Yet she wanted to know more about his life. Shaletha finally decided to let the conversation take its own course without trying to direct it as she had done before.

"Hy!" She said as a start.

"Hy!" Answered Adrian.

"Is the bed too short for you?"

"No, it's fine, and very fluffy."

The pointless conversation continued to flow and it was obvious that both were comfortable with it.

"... What's up? Did I say the wrong thing?" Asked Shaletha at a time due to the lack of response from him.

"Quite the opposite. I shut up simply because I like to hear your voice."

Guided by an impulse Shaletha, who had sat on the bed, leaned over and kissed the man's lips, but this time it was not a kiss burning with passion, but a sweet and gentle kiss.

"I liked that." He said quietly.

"You need to shave, your chin is rough." Answered Shaletha diverting the subject to control her own feelings. The young man took her by the waist and gently laid her beside him. They stayed silent with their heads together. Shaletha felt she was falling in love for the first time in her life.

After sleeping until 3 pm they had lunch eating the food the food Shaletha had prepared herself for the next few days as she returned from her job. They ate in silence, knowing that the time Adrian had to leave to get ready for work the next day approached. On one hand Shaletha wanted to postpone that moment as much as possible but in her heart she recognized the need to spend time alone to process everything that happened in the past 24 hours.

Upon retiring man kissed the hostess, as he said.

"Everything they say about black women is true. Today I have fulfilled all my erotic fantasies."

"I hope not only for that reason."

"Time will prove that is not all. You know what they say also."

"What do they say?"

"That being for the first time with a black woman is a road of no return."

"I'll make sure that you do not return anywhere without me."

Arionna´s eyes were wide open.

"Four times in one night! I wonder how you ended up."

Shaletha could not help blushing. She expected such a comment of her friend although she knew that her sarcasm was well-intentioned.

"This exceeds my experience with Kevin." Went on Arionna. " Is there something stronger than Viagra?"

Shaletha could not help laughing out loud and Arionna joined him as she held her hand.

"You cannot imagine how happy this makes me, especially for taking part in rushing your decision. Tell me, did you consider my advice to demand oral sex before."

Shaletha was quick to answer.

"No need, as sooner as we entered my apartment he pounced on me and ..."

The woman stopped as she realized that her tongue had run out of her control; her face flushed again.

"¡Arionna. Look at the things that you make me say!"

" Come on woman, releasing everything is good for you. You are telling your best friend about your big moment. I see that this Adrian knows his duties towards a woman. I want every detail."

Once Shaletha had exhaustively answered her questions Arionna thought for a moment and added.

"Next time must not allow that rush. You must make him worship your whole body before, and when I say whole I mean every part of it. Now listen, I need to know this boy. Invite him to dinner with my husband and me. I really care about Kevin´s opinion. Being a teacher he is very used to assess young people. Meanwhile, you'll come to dinner with us tonight. I want that you also hear his opinion.

Arionna opened the door as soon as Shaletha rang the house doorbell. It was obvious that the hostess had waiting for her friend. The two women breathed calm, both had individually decided to attend the meeting well dressed.

"Here, put this in the fridge right away, it is an ice cream." Said Shaletha.

"All right. Come in. Kevin is in the living room."

The visitor, obviously familiar with the house left her purse on a shelf, hung her coat on a hook, crossed the lobby and entered the room. Kevin rose from his chair and walked over to kiss her on the cheek. He was a big man, about forty-five, with red thinning hair and beard. If Arionna and Shaletha had tacitly agreed to meet smartly dressed, Kevin had obviously not been notified. He was dressed in tattered jeans, sandals and a shirt that had seen better days. But it did not matter, because the contest was just about feminine outfits and did not involve him, so he did not take the hint.

When they had finished eating the dessert with her usual straightforward style Arionna decided to cut to the chase. She addressed her husband.

"Shaletha has met a boy she likes and apparently likes her. They have had a torrid first appointment, to call it in some way. But she is now struggling with her inner demons by lying with a younger white man who is also an illegal immigrant. In short, Shaletha has decided to add milk to her coffee and feels bad about it."

Hearing such a crude but accurate description of her problem Shaletha wished the earth swallowed her; yet she knew that that she would come out of this meeting with her conflicts clarified at least in part, as she would have an opinion of two people who loved her and would not be obscured by the emotional block that the issue was obviously causing her.

Kevin thought for a moment looking for the tip of the iceberg in order to address the problem, and then gave his opinion in an organized way.

"Though some pockets of racism still remain, the situation of ethnic minorities in this country and in most of the world is objectively better. In the black people there's even an awakening of the concept of Africa as a unit, unfortunately obscured by intertribal warfare that still remains."

He paused and took a sip of tea.

"But at the level of individual and collective behavior there are still in our country and elsewhere many remnants, more typical of ghettos that of an open and plural society, and many people persist in their legitimate protests and claims but have not changed their minds. This can be seen in older generations that currently have problems understanding what goes through the head of their children and grandchildren."

Kevin stared at Shaletha eyes.

"In what concerns you, the truth is you cannot avoid this conflict, especially coming from a traditional Harlem family." He made a pause again looking for the best words to continue his reasoning that was definitely entering in its final phase.

"Only you are responsible for your happiness and to achieve it you must counteract some very strong opinions of your loved ones. It will be a way you will have to walk by yourself, but of course your friends are here to support you. The barriers between ethnic groups that have always existed are crumbling and it is this generation that will carry the weight that comes with the change and the corresponding suffering, but it is the price of large scale deliverance that is under way."

"Why do not you speak of the specific case that concerns Shaletha that is the relationships between black women and white men." Asked Arionna who was listening Kevin's words as attentively as Shaletha who nodded showing interest.

"For centuries since both races got in contact the white man was the owner of the body and the fate of the black women and men and in times of slavery used them at will. But that time is over and now young people are looking each other with new eyes as they are not judging by the weight of that unhappy historical burden. And what they see is that there is more physical attraction and greater emotional closeness between a part of black women and white men than with their counterparts of their own racial groups. I have experienced firsthand what I am now saying. What is happening is that girls and boys are opening up to the new reality, and reality is liberating because it gives them a very large freedom of choice."

"White boys are ready to open themselves to the extent that they see that black girls are also open to them." Added Arionna" The ball is now in the court of the girls, and is being set in motion as evidenced by social networks full of groups advocating these relationships.

"What about Asian girls?" Asked Shaletha. "They also came as poor immigrants, often not speaking the language yet marry our men quite frequently."

"It's true." Recognized Arionna. "One of the complaints of black women is that men will seek wives in Asia and not in their own neighborhood, that is to say the girl next door."

"What happens is that although they arrived relatively recently as poor immigrants and that the cultural gap is greater than in the case of African Americans, Asians were never subject in our country to the stigma of slavery." Answered Kevin. "It shows the weight of past relationships and social taboos in matchmaking that can prevail even over physical attraction. It's a pretty crazy but well proven fact."

The conversation lasted a bit longer. Shaletha felt that her friends' explanations were convincing and that certain knots deep inside her were beginning to loosen. Suddenly and for no apparent reason she began to cry. Arionna solicitously approached Shaletha to calm her but Kevin held her hand.

"Let her vent. Apparently this whole situation with her family and her past had produced her a very large internal stress that now begins to relax. These are liberating tears."

CHAPTER 6

AS OUTSIDE IT WAS POURING Shaletha quickly opened the house door since she figured that Adrian was getting drenched. She let him enter the lobby where the young man took off his wet jacket.

"Take off also your shoes." Said the woman. "They are soaked and if you keep your feet wet you will get sick."

"But I will not walk barefoot in the living room."

"I'll bring some of my slippers. Although they will be small for you at least you can walk."

Sitting in front of two cups of coffee the young couple stayed silent for a while. Finally Shaletha, who was dressed to go out together that Saturday evening said.

"The rain will not cease. We will not be able to go out today."

Going to the theater as they had planned effectively involved walking many blocks underwater to take the subway and on the other side getting a taxi in Brooklyn Heights with that weather would not be easy, even with radio taxis.

"If we have to stay here together I won´t complain". Said Adrian with a mischievous gesture. "Come sit with me on the couch."

"Wait. I'll change my clothes into something more suitable."

Shaletha went to her bedroom while the man wandered his eyes looking at the contents of the living room. She returned after a few minutes with her outfit completely changed. She wore very short and tight pants that revealed her fleshy thighs and beautiful knees, and allowed the man to guess her prominent rear. A soft cloth shirt had only three buttons fastened and its tails knotted at her waist; in her feet she only wore sandals. She sat in the three- seats coach on the opposite end where Adrian was, so that they were separated by a certain distance.

"Holy God! You are beautiful." Exclaimed the man as he tried to crawl on the couch to approach her. Shaletha turned her body facing him and lifted one leg, placing the sole of her foot on his face slowing his momentum.

"Stop, stop! I will not withstand again a testosterone hurricane again. I'm the one with the treasure to be conquered and I will set the game rules."

"What do you mean?"

"I am a beautiful and desirable woman. From now on I will control the situation and will mark time. I want to be conquered inch by inch and I 'll indicate what I like and things I do not like. Do you accept the rules?"

"Ye...Yes, of course." Adrian's face showed however a certain mistrust.

She started touring down the man's face with her toes, beginning on his forehead, eyes, and nose and when reaching his mouth she forced it open and introduced her foot inside. Adrian understood the game and followed suit. He kissed the foot and then introduced his tongue between her fingers. When she pulled his foot out of his mouth he continued kissing her ankles and continued its upward march.

Shaletha was in the middle of a drowsiness produced by the pleasure. She was with the man she had chosen, had already fiercely mated with him last week and was now giving vent to her sexual fantasies, that lately during some nights rendered it difficult to sleep. Adrian ran that perfect body sparingly and after reaching the breasts retreated placing his face in front of the short pants. He looked into the Shaletha´s eyes and she nodded. The boy pulled the shorts and panties and approached his face to the Mount of Venus.

"I warn you that I feel wet out of excitement."

"Do not worry. I'll take care."

The woman was riding her man's face and did it slowly, prolonging the time while stored in her memory all the feelings and sensations she was experiencing. Finally, from some place far away and deep an orgasm emerged that immediately turned into a gale.

"The dark side of this is what you will do to surprise me the next time."She said.

"Don´t worry. I´ll think of something."

"Tell me something about you. I already have told you everything about my life as a child and teenager in Harlem, my time in high school and college, the fleeting romances I had and about problems in my family, but I know almost nothing about you. You could be a drug dealer or terrorist or something."

"Well, I'm not."

"Tell me then you really are."

"My childhood in my home town was pretty dull, as often happens in small towns. There I made the primary and secondary school, and then I moved to Buenos Aires to pursue my studies at the Faculty of Architecture, Planning and Design."

"There you surely have met many girls."

"A few future architects. When I graduated a couple of years ago, I realized I had spent enough time studying locked in a small rented room and decided to travel around for a while before going back and settling down. I was first in Rio de Janeiro until somewhat suddenly I decided to come to New York."

"Did you live in Rio de Janeiro?"

"Yes. If I found a good job there it would be my place in the world. I love the light-hearted atmosphere and gracious living."

"What about women in Rio?"

"It was in Rio where I acquired a preference for black women."

"But you said you had the intention to return to your country."

"But then New York crossed my path."

" Is just New York holding you back?"

"New York and now a New Yorker."

Shaletha passed her beautiful foot along his face again.

"Go on flattering me. I really like it."

"You like it or it excites you?"

"What's the difference?"

Shaletha was quite busy in office when her cell phone rang. On the screen appeared a family picture.

"Hi, Arionna! How are you?"

" Well, and how was your second appointment with your hero." Arionna never lost time.

Shaletha pleased squirmed in her chair.

"Better than the first, if that were possible."

" Did you take control as I advised."

"You do not really expect me to tell you what happened. I am working."

"Well, listen, Kevin and I have decided to invite to dinner you and your friend, lover or whatever he is."

"I see you are really curious about him." Shaletha was obviously flattered.

"I cannot wait to see him. Is it okay Thursday at nine pm?"

"I'm going to invite him. I guess it'll be all right."

Adrian passed by Shaletha's apartment and both walked together to the place where Arionna and her husband lived, a few blocks distant. They were walking arm in arm and talking in very good spirits as they had to stop at a corner waiting the red traffic light to turn green when an old elegantly dressed woman, very thin and wrinkled and with big blue eyes unexpectedly addressed the man in a stern tone.

"Young man. You are giving a deplorable spectacle exhibiting yourself publicly with this woman ... of different ethnicity. You will contribute to keep filling this nation with mixed race children."

Adrian's face turned red. While Shaletha pulled his arm to carry him away from that place the man gulped, tried to compose his attitude and answered in a low, controlled voice.

"Lady, with all due respect. My ethnicity and the color of my future children are not your business."

The lady stared at him and followed her course with an aggrieved gesture.

"This is incredible! Why does that meddlesome old woman dare to get into my personal life and rebuke me for my personal choices in the street and in the light of day."

"Let´s move on. This gives you an idea of what we have suffered for generations in this country." Shaletha tugged his arm again and stroked the boy's head in a gesture of comfort.

"Look, here we are; this is Arionna´s house."

"So this is the famous Adrian! Come inside."

The young man kissed the woman´s cheek, who was a little surprised and said, laughing.

"Well, if Shaletha doesn´t mind it!"

"In his country they have the habit of kissing women they just met." Answered also laughing Shaletha. "At least this is the story he told me."

"Excuse me ... was an involuntary act." Said somewhat embarrassed Adrian. "True, I have lost the habit of shaking hands with a woman."

"Well, it's a kind of gesture that perhaps we should imitate in this country." Replied the hostess. "Let me take care of your coat."

Arionna led them to the living room, where Kevin who was sitting in a couch immediately stood up to greet the newcomers.

"And your name is ...?" Asked Arionna.

"Ah! Yes ... sorry. I'm Adrian Bianchi."

"Adrian is a bit upset. We just had an unpleasant episode, which has affected him more than it should have." Explained Shaletha, and then narrated what happened in the street with the old lady.

"I'm sorry and ashamed that these things still happen in America." Said Kevin putting familiarly a hand on the young man's shoulder. At the beginning we had a couple of similar episodes with Arionna, but they are now increasingly becoming scarce. I have to add that in our case we were always criticized also by white women."

"They hate competition from blacks." Arionna added with her usual cheerful tone." Those disdainful and ungainly women cannot take care of their men and seek out culprits."

"Let´s forget this episode. Come and sit down." Kevin pointed the way towards the couches.

"You come with me to the kitchen to help me out." Said Arionna addressing her friend.

" He is good looking..." Said once they were in the kitchen. "..And young. Dear, I'm happy for you. You deserve no less. What did he say his name is?"

"Bianchi. Adrian Bianchi."

"So ultimately this is another case of black woman with Italian man romance. Chocolate with red wine. It is a proven and successful mixture."

"Can´t you be serious for once?" Shaletha said in mock anger.

After a short time the conversation turned to Argentina that logically was a topic of interest for the hosts, both by the novelty and the fact that Kevin was a professor of history.

"Is it true that in Argentina there are no black people?" Asked the hostess.

"Actually in the streets you see very few and they are generally foreigners. There are many more Eastern than African descendants."

"I know that Argentina is a country of immigration, like the United States or Canada." Expressed Kevin. "It is odd that there is no population of African origin. Didn´t they bring slaves at the time of the Spanish colony, as the Portuguese brought to Brazil?"

"Perhaps the quantity was much smaller. Due to weather in what is now Argentina there were no huge plantations of cotton, coffee or the like. But history tells that in the colonial times a sizeable part of the Buenos Aires population were African slaves."

"Interesting." Said Kevin moving in his chair so that his body revealed he was paying attention. "What happened to them?"

"On one side they fought in the wars of independence from 1810 on . The 1813 the Assembly of year XIII, one of the precedents of the Argentine Constitution enacted the so-called "freedom of wombs"." Said Adrian.

"What does that mean?"Asked Arionna. "The end of slavery?"

"Not yet. It meant free birth, that is everybody in the country was born free, even if he or she was born of to a slave mother. Freedom was granted when they got married or on the 16th birthday, whichever happened first."

"So that the children of black women were born free, although their mothers were still slaves." Asked again the hostess." Weren´t the white masters just freeing their own half caste children?"

"In some cases it may true." Answered Adrian." But the result was that when the Constitution was promulgated in 1853 including the end of slavery there were actually very few slaves."

"'Actually both 1813 and 1853 predated the Emancipation Proclamation in 1863 in our country by President Abraham Lincoln after the Civil War. And the slave trade had been outlawed in the British Empire from 1807. Argentina was then one of the pioneer countries in this regard." Meditated Kevin. "Perhaps the fact that there were no large plantations or mines in the territory meant that there were no major economic interests linked to the existence of slaves." He paused and then asked. "How did Argentina become an agricultural and cattle growing power?"

"Open fields' livestock existed since the colonial times. Extensive farming appears with the great European immigration from 1870 onwards."

"What happened to the blacks who were already in the country?" Asked Arionna.

"There were major pests in Buenos Aires during the nineteenth century. The yellow fever ravaged the city, especially the poor neighborhoods inhabited by black people. Civil wars and especially the bloody war with Paraguay also produced many casualties."

"And certainly the black were in the first line."Argued Arionna.

"I know that they participated in the wars precisely because they were free men." Replied the young man.

"Freedom has its price." Mused Kevin.

"'And then what happened?" Insisted obviously interested his wife. Meanwhile Shaletha was in an obviously attentive attitude.

"From the beginning of the great wave of immigration from 1853 and throughout the rest of the nineteenth century consisted mostly of single males so there was a great ethnic mixture. The immigrants outnumbered the natives by far."

Kevin had opened his notebook and was doing a Google search under the terms "mestizaje en Argentina" in Spanish.

"Pay attention to this." He translated. "According to genetic studies by gender, paternal genetic contribution in Argentina's population reveals approximately 94% of European component, 5% of indigenous and 1% African. Maternal contributions instead are 44% European, 54%% indigenous and 2% African. This caused that indigenous and African ethnic features got diluted in the European tide."

"Summing up Europeans massively interbred with Indian and black women." Briefly summarized Arionna. "I wonder if it happened voluntarily." Added with her usual vindictive tone.

"Nobody forced you and me to choose white men." Shaletha's tone was of friendly reproach.

"I do not think anyone has forced women to marry the immigrants." Said Adrian. "They could have done it by their own free will ..."

" ... Or to move up the social ladder."Concluded the homeowner.

"Most of the immigrants were very poor and had a low status in the society of that time." Insisted the young man.

Arionna raised the forefinger of her right hand; her general attitude anticipated that what she was about to add would be one of her ironic comments.

"I have to admit that for many black girls I know it would have been an ideal situation. They would have had plenty of candidates to choose."

Her husband burst out laughing.

" Anyway. What this study shows is that the indigenous ethnic component is very strong in Argentina and the African is there, but it is not obvious to the naked eye." Concluded Kevin.

" So the couple formed by you two has many precedents in your country." Said Arionna said addressing his visitors. "Despite whatever the old silly lady you met in Brooklyn Heights has to say."

The meeting was coming to an end since the following day everyone had to go to work.

"What we have learned today about your country is very interesting." Said Kevin as he shook his visitor′s hand. "We have to meet again sometime soon."

"Thanks for the hospitality, Kevin. Since I arrived in New York I had not been invited to such a nice meeting."

As they left Arionna′s house Adrian walked Shaletha home.

"Don′t you want to stay tonight?" Asked she.

"I have to get up early tomorrow and you know that I have a long trip. Besides it′ll soon be weekend."

"You are right. Come on Saturday morning and bring staff to spend two days with me."

"Some invitation! Big challenge for me."

"I must squeeze you well."

"Am I a lemon or something like that?"

"Something like that."

Taking advantage that nobody was passing by on the street, they joined in a long passionate kiss.

" That´s enough! Otherwise I will not be able to sleep this night." Exclaimed the woman.

Shaletha had already gone to bed when her cell phone rang.

"Hello Arionna." She said yawning as she recognized the picture on the screen.

"I wanted to tell you that your boy has produced an excellent impression on Kevin and on me." Whoever knew her could immediately recognize her tone was serious.

"I'm glad. A kiss."

Shaletha returned to bed and despite her fears fell immediately deeply asleep.

CHAPTER 7

THE TWO BOYS WALKED unsteadily down the alley, singing in loud and out of tune voices despite being in the middle of the night, kicking garbage cans in their path and picking and throwing on the walls beer cans and other things scattered on the dirty floor. The fear of the neighbors to open their windows to the outer darkness full of dangers and threats and accepting suffering in silence had assured the youngsters a high degree of impunity. That part of Harlem had not experienced yet the positive changes that had made the life of most of its inhabitants safer and more pleasant.

The effect of alcohol and other substances was certainly evident in the aggressive behavior of the boys and in the incoherent babbling when speaking and singing.

"Hey Leroy! Look at that bottle there. Let's blow it into a thousand pieces."

The other boy placed the empty bottle found in a pile of garbage on one of the waste containers and both started throwing stones and other objects on it until they finally broke into pieces that fell noisily on the ground. The laughter followed the crash and the vandals hugged each other crying of joy and drunkenness.

"Hey Zion! Where does that light come from?"

"If some neighbor opened the window he'll damn regret it."

"No, look. The light comes from the corner."

Indeed, once the man called Leroy partially covered his eyes with his hands he could see the dazzling light coming from the headlights of a car approaching from the corner they had just left.

"It's a trap Zion. Run!"

With their minds suddenly cleared by the imminent danger the two boys ran in the opposite direction only to find that in the other corner also the powerful headlights of a car parked in it lit up shedding on them a morning clarity.

"We're in a rat trap." Cried desperately Leroy. At that time the shooting began from the first car.

"Help me Zion! They got me."

Leroy was slowly collapsing to the ground; his abdomen showed dark spots and Zion guessed what they were. Leroy was laboriously pulling something out of his clothing but eventually his movements stopped. Zion took in his trembling hands the 38 Smith & Wesson that he knew his friend was always carrying. Terrified he verified that the first car had stopped and from it descended a giant black man carrying in his hands what he could make out as a rifle.

Zion did not hesitate, while the bully pointed at him he raised the gun and fired a lucky shot that hit the forehead of his rival, who collapsed without a whimper. Zion jumped like a spring and ran at full speed towards the first car emptying the magazine of his gun on the vehicle. As he passed he could see that the riddled windshield showed large bloodstains. Looking inside the vehicle Zion recognized the driver, a member of a rival gang; the man was obviously dead.

From the other car came loud cries and as he turned around Zion distinguished three heavily armed black men walking in his direction. He ran desperately for his life and despite the burden of alcohol and narcotics he had in his body he could put enough distance from his pursuers and get lost in the jungle of shadowy alleys. His heart was pounding from the exertion and terror. He knew perfectly well who were chasing him and why. He had now killed two of them and was sure that it would only increase their hatred and would multiply the means to pursue him. He erased the traces of the revolver in his shirt and tossed it into a street drain. His brain riddled with drugs was desperately seeking a way out.

Shaletha woke startled by the sound of the cell phone.

"Damn cell. I forgot to turn it off last night. Who can be calling at this hour? I just fell asleep." She thought angrily. Then she glanced at the alarm clock and saw it was four in the morning.

"Hello. Zion! What happens to you? I do not understand. Are you high? ... What are you saying? ... Oh my God! ... You say that you killed two men?"

Shaletha sat on the floor because she felt her legs would not hold her. She kept listening to the babbling explanations of her brother, who usually had slurred speech, and now, under the influence of drugs and terror only managed to utter incoherent grunts.

"Where are you now? ... Yes, I remember the place. It is a scary place full of danger ... Well, stay there, I will see that I can think of."

Her brother had been a kind of permanent sentence in Shaletha's life, but had never reached such extremes before. Now he had killed human beings and was being sought by one of the most dangerous drug gangs in New York that sought to assassinate him.

The girl immediately dismissed the idea of ignoring a problem that was not truly hers and that was wrapped in risks.

"Blood is thicker than water." She thought.

Shaletha's head was spinning around, so she rose to warm some coffee looking to clear her mind. Indeed, the overheated and strong brew made her react and could finally develop a plan. The woman took the phone and searched a number in the device memory.

"Adrian, I'm Shaletha ... No, no, I'm fine. Forgive me for calling you at half past four, but I do not know where else to turn. Listen to me please. My brother Zion just called me. I told before you that he is involved in drug distribution problems with a gang of Harlem dealers. ... He just told me he is being sought by the thugs of a rival gang to assassinate him by a matter of territorial dispute." Although she could not rationally explain why Shaletha decided to skip the murder confession that her brother had done. "He is hiding in Harlem in a place where we used to play when we were children... and asks me to go find him... something like the "extractions" in spy movies... Hi ...Are you still there?"

"Yes, Shaletha, I'm just thinking. This situation is also new to me ... Listen, I'll borrow a car to my Puerto Rican work fellow who lives downstairs. Get ready because I ′ll pick you ...I do not know how long it will take, I have to go to your apartment from Queens, but I estimate that at this time I will not find a lot of traffic. Can you communicate with your brother?"

"I think that the number from which he called me should be in the register of my phone."

"Well, get ready to go."

Shaletha managed to catch her breath to get moving after the news that had awakened her. The woman ′s head was still running fast.

"Hell, it ′s his son after all. I ′ve got to call him. "

Shaletha dialed another number in the cell and soon heard her father ′s alarmed voice.

"Shaletha dear. What's happening to you?"

The woman repeated to her father the entire conversation with Zion and then with Adrian.

"...Good God. You say he killed two men?"

"From what he said it was self-defense. We would not be talking about him now if he had not shot first."

" And you say that you first called your boyfriend rather than your father."

"I called who I knew was going to give me an answer. I'm sorry Dad, you're part of Zion ′s problem . What you should be asking yourself is not why I called my friend before calling you. You ought to ask yourself why your son called me and not you in his time of despair."

Shaletha heard a moan on the other side of the line.

"Can I count on you to find Zion?"

"Of course daughter."

"All right. Get ready. Adrian will first pick me up at my house and then we will pick you. The place where we should look for Zion is not far from your home."

The old Toyota stopped and double-parked in the place indicated by Shaletha.

"Wait for us with the engine running. I will go bring my father ... No! There he is leaving the house."

The old man got into the car and Shaletha made the introductions. Ezra Moore knew that her daughter's boyfriend was white and expected to meet him; yet his stomach knotted as he shook his hand.

"The car door on your side does not close well, Mr. Moore. Please make sure it's close."

"Call me Ezra." Said the father slamming the door as required.

"All right Ezra. I am Adrian." The boy turned in the driver's seat and told his two companions.

"Shaletha gets down right here and waits for our return. I will not let her run any dangers. It is my condition to move forward."

"No way ..." The woman began to whisper."

Ezra put a hand on her shoulder.

"Daughter, Adrian is absolutely right. Tell me where to find Zion and get off the car. What you can do is to call him and explain that we are on our way and then you wait for us at home." Shaletha noticed a determination tone in her father's voice that she had not heard for a long time before and decided not to waste any more time in useless discussions.

"Well Dad. Good luck to both."

As they drove the blocks that separated the place where they were heading Ezra said.

"As I was waiting for Shaletha and you I phoned my older brother. He lives in Gary, Indiana, where he was a cop for thirty years. He is also Zion's godfather and always took that responsibility seriously, although it also brought him suffering. He developed a plan to get Zion temporarily out of his problem. We cannot count on passing him through airports and bus terminals because the drug bands will have them controlled. We must carry the boy to Albany. Are you willing to take that risk?"

"I will, since I am involved already in this affair."

"Meanwhile my brother Jacob is organizing a transport truck to drive Zion from Albany to Gary. It is a city near Chicago and is inhabited mostly by black people. The New York bands have no place there. They will keep the boy hidden for a while and whenever they can they'll take him out of the country."

Jacob had asked his brother if his niece's boyfriend was to be trusted and Ezra had to confess he did not know him, but he entirely trusted in his daughter's judgment.

"Does Shaletha's boyfriend know that Zion has killed two men?" Asked Jacob.

"He does not. For reasons that are not even clear to her Shaletha has not told him."

"It's better that way. The less he knows the better. Besides it does not make sense to involve him in a criminal offense such as giving assistance to an escaped killer. We are family and we have a discharge, but it is not his case."

But Ezra did not tell Adrian this part of the conversation.

Once at the site indicated by Shaletha Adrian stopped the vehicle.

"Stay in the car." said Ezra." The boy must be terrified and he should only see faces known to him." The man descended from the car and entered an abandoned building by opening a door that creaked horribly. The boy looked at him walking with difficult movements to fetch his son gone astray; he could not prevent a certain admiration for the old man's determination.

Adrian remained in the vehicle and watched apprehensively at the few pedestrians who happened to pass by that forgotten alley to satisfy God knows what necessities. He was in turn regarded with suspicion and hostility by walkers who did not understand that was an unknown white boy doing inside a car with the engine running in their neighborhood. A young black man who was passing by hit the glass of the passenger window while shouting something incomprehensible to Adrian. With his objective mind the boy could not help understanding and even sympathizing with the neighbor´s behavior.

He took his phone and made a call to his friend and colleague warning him not to expect the car back until the next day.

"No problem. I will not use until next weekend. Just bring it back without any damage."

"Thanks Manuel. I owe you one."

Due to the tension waiting seemed eternal and Adrian noticed his hands were sweaty despite the cold morning.

Ezra finally appeared pulling a ragged boy moving in a shaky way. It was evident that the father had been waiting for a time at the building door until no bystander was at sight to minimize the potential leakage to the persecutors of news about his son.

"Who is this white boy?" Squealed Zion.

"He's Shaletha´s boyfriend. Get in the car, I do not want anybody to see us. Go in the back seat and throw yourself on the floor. No one should see you from here to Albany."

"It´s a160 miles ride!"

"You have no choice, unless you want to go in the trunk." Was the harsh rebuke.

The trip down the broad highway was pretty fast. At one point Adrian saw in the distance several policemen on both sides of the road.

"Look. They are stopping the traffic."

"It cannot be related to Zion. Nobody can relate our trip in this highway with a crime in Harlem. Just slow down and see what happens." Answered Ezra turning toward the backseat and accommodating several coats covering the body of Zion who was fast asleep. As the boy snored Ezra turned on the car radio and set it to the maximum volume.

The policeman with a hand signal indicated them to stop by the roadside.

"Have you got the car papers and a valid driver's license?" Asked Ezra, while Adrian nodded affirmatively.

The police approached the car and asked the driver to open his window. Adrian had prepared the documents in his hand and intended to hand them over to the trooper.

"No need." Replied the officer. "This is not a route control. We just want to alert you that there is a tank truck loaded with chemicals overturned a mile ahead... Jesus, could you please lower the volume of the radio."

"Yes, sorry." Replied Adrian." My father-in-law is a bit deaf."

Ezra trembled as he thought that his son could emit untimely sounds but fortunately nothing happened.

"Very well sir, have a good day." Replied the officer, as he signed them to move on.

Ezra drew a long sigh of relief; Zion just then turned still asleep on the floor of the car and started coughing loudly. Just one minute before...!

"What is that deaf father-in-law business?"

"Well, we needed to muddle through somehow and it worked."

Ezra thought he maybe should get used to the idea of being an in-law, even of a white man.

"Well, I'm not deaf." Mumbled.

The rest of the trip to Albany had no further alternatives. Ezra received a call from his brother, giving the name and address of the person who was waiting for them in the city, actually in the suburbs. As they arrived the old man came down the car, rang the house doorbell and was let in. After a while the gate of a garage belonging to the house opened and a black man waved Adrian to enter the car in it. The door closed behind them and Adrian saw Ezra already waiting inside the garage. He leaned into the car and told his son to come out. The boy did so grumbling by the position that had endured for three hours.

"Don´t complain." Answered grimly the father. "Were it not been for you and your relationships we would not be going through this."

Zion was unmoved and answered.

"You can tell Shaletha her whitey ... cool."

What likely was the longest and more complex sentence he uttered in a week.

On the return trip and Adrian and Ezra kept silent for much of the way. The old man's eyes were red and it was evident that all sorts of gloomy thoughts hovered his mind. At one point he began to mourn in silence. Without a word Adrian took a hand off the wheel and placed it on Ezra´s.

CHAPTER 8

SHALETHA HEARD HER cell phone ringing and took the call. She was glad that it was Arionna who was calling. After a day of torment and extreme stress the woman needed someone to talk to relieve her tensions and she could not think of a better balm than her friend.

Arionna did not try to calm down Shaletha from the beginning, she knew her well and realized that her best friend needed to remove all the anguish from her body and her mind. Only once she considered that catharsis had taken place her natural empathy began to play.

"I understand all the pain you brother and his situation are causing you, but think that he turned to you in his most desperate moment and despite your lack of preparation for such circumstances you answered properly and together with your boyfriend and your relatives you have been able to avoid at least the more imminent danger. The best you could have done with Zion was to take him out of the environment in which he was living and give him a chance elsewhere. In due time he will have to face his legal situation. Do you know where he will go?"

"When the waters calm down uncle Jacob will have Zion make an overseas trip from Chicago, but we do not know where."

"It's better this way ... There is another topic that you must think about."

"What do you mean?"

"Everybody in your environment was put on high voltage and responded well even though they were not prepared for handling such a situation either. In particular Adrian, who threw himself into a risky situation, despite not being part of the family and of his illegal status.

It is a practical demonstration of his love for you that otherwise you would not have had."

"As usual you're right."

"And also the situation has allowed your father to do something concrete for his son, something he had not done before."

Arionna´s comforting words had the paradoxical effect of making her friend burst into tears. The woman allowed her to let all the steam off before she continued talking.

"In the midst of so much drama, I have good news to share with you."

"What is it about?"

"I'm pregnant."

Shaletha screamed.

"Oh! Arionna, that's wonderful. This fulfills your dreams of the last years.

"The dreams of my whole life."

The change that the news produced in Shaletha´s mood was so abrupt that her friend smiled at her image in a mirror. Actually her call had the purpose of sharing with Shaletha the news of her pregnancy, but upon learning of the situation traversed by her in relation with her brother Arionna had patiently waited for the right time to take her friend's emotional state out of the deep well where it was. Arionna was self-satisfied with the results of her psychological evaluation.

The conversation then led to Kevin reaction as he learned about the pregnancy and other issues, and when they cut the communication Shaletha had the perception that the dark episode related to Zion had began to be buried in the past.

The doorbell rang. The woman rushed to open and through the peephole confirmed that was indeed Adrian who had arrived. She opened the door, took his hand and without any word dragged him from the hall to the bedroom. There she pushed him on the bed and said.

"Adrian Bianchi. I will make love to you as no one has in your life and as only a black woman can do."

Exhausted and sweaty both lay in bed without the energy to get up. Shaletha had already offered to prepare dinner together but he was still gathering strength.

"You probably don't know it but you've become a hero to my father. Imagine, a stranger appeared out of nowhere to help him solve the biggest mess that his family was involved in its existence. So he has even forgotten the color of your skin."

"Bah! I think the hero who actually gave the solution was that Jacob from Mary, Indiana."

"Gary, Indiana. Yes, Uncle Jake is and has always been kind of a guardian angel of the family, but the one who drew up the pieces until Jake could take action was you."

Shaletha could finally decide to get out of bed and put on a robe.

"Ah! Another important news. Arionna is pregnant."

"So they have achieved what they have been looking for in years. I am delighted with the news ..."

"But?"

"But what?"

"But I have the perception that you envy her, even a little." Adrian tone was between a statement and a question. Shaletha intended to get finally out of bed, but the man grabbed her arm and pulled her back on the bed.

"Do you know? We could do something about it." Said he while kissing her in the mouth and inserting his hands in her clothes.

"Well, I can see that even after the trip to Albany you are not hungry."

Adrian returned from his work at 7 pm. The night before he had stayed in Shaletha's apartment, and although they had not decided it yet he would possibly do the same that night. After the shower he left the bathroom still partially clothed. Adrian found that Shaletha was setting the table.

"What have you ordered for today?" He asked.

" Today I also ordered Chinese food but tomorrow I promise to cook for you."

"I cannot stay another day. I am wearing the same shirt that I had when we went to Albany. I need to see what happens in my apartment, letters, accounts payable and stuff."

"But you receive and pay everything through Internet." Shaletha looked cuddly as she was hugging him. " I think that you do not want to be with me anymore."

"You know that the truth is exactly the opposite."

"Fine, but if you go home bring clothes for several days."

"A tempting proposition."

"Ah! I almost forgot to tell you. My father has invited us to dinner at his house on Saturday."

"With your father we have already reached a coexistence agreement, but what about your mother?"

"You've hit the nail. That is the issue. Meanwhile my sister is anxious to meet you. She likes young white boys and in fact has a Russian friend. This drives my mother crazy."

" I do not think that for her an Argentine friend will be any better than a Russian one."

"It's probably so. Do you dare to be exposed to that?"

"If I dared to go find your brother I guess I can face your mother."

On Saturday they traveled by subway and got off at the 125th Street station . Almost all train passengers and those who they found in the mezzanine of the station were black people. Shaletha insisted on going arm in arm with Adrian, despite the hostile looks of some men, but they were only addressed by an African American elderly lady who told them.

"You make a beautiful couple, and I am pleased to see you. In my time I had a white boyfriend in Mississippi but we had to meet in secret."

They walked several blocks down a side street and suddenly a young man began to gesticulate and shout from the opposite sidewalk. Shaletha had an unexpected reaction, crossed the street and stood before him and rebuked him in terms that Adrian could not understand. The man, taken aback lowered his head and slipped out from the scene while all the passers followed him with their eyes.

When Shaletha returned her boyfriend asked.

"What happened? What was that boy screaming to us?"

"He was calling you "pale demon" and asking you to leave the "sisters" alone."

"Who do you think he is?"

"One of those African Americans who believe that black women are their exclusive hunting ground."

"Some sultan or caliph mentality. And were you not afraid of going to face him?"

" This is the neighborhood where I was born and raised, I will not let some coward clown frighten me. There was also you." She took his arm back. "Tell me what would you have done if I was attacked?"

"Running away, no doubt. What else did you expect with so many blacks around."

Shaletha pinched his arm as she let out a burst of laughter.

"You just have to watch out of this black."

"Too late for that."

"You would do a good match with Arionna."

"I would have first to consult with Kevin, who just made a major investment in her belly."

"I'm talking about your sarcasm, silly. Look, we have already arrived."

Ezra opened the door, embraced and kissed his daughter and shook hands with Adrian.

On entering the house they met a beautiful girl. Shaletha made the introductions.

"Alyssa, this is Adrian. Adrian she is Alyssa. Is she not a beauty?"

" She's really beautiful." Answered the man and then addressing the father. " Ezra, I congratulate you on your two daughters."

"So you're the "famous" Adrian." Said Alyssa. "Well, no wonder Shaletha has hidden you so well."

"Alyssa, don't be so bold. I saw him first." Exclaimed her sister.

At that time a woman came into the lobby and the festive atmosphere that had prevailed until then was put on hold.

"Mom, this is my boyfriend Adrian. Adrian, my mother."

The young man noticed that the mother's stern face had an imperceptible twitch at the word "boyfriend". Otherwise it was obvious that she had passed on her beauty to their daughters.

"Madam." Said stretching her hand.

"I'm Helen Moore." She shook hands and immediately turned around. "Please come in to the living room.

In the chatter that preceded the dinner Alyssa took almost permanently the initiative. Actually she was the closest in age to the visitor and asked all kinds of questions about the teenagers living in Argentina, many of which went unanswered.

"Alyssa, do not overwhelm Adrian with your questions." Kindly reprimanded Ezra, who was attentively watching the scene. "Obviously he is not aware of all your bands, artists, heroes and villains."

It was evident that Alyssa had a strong musical inclination and was very up to date on the subject. She finally asked.

"What kind of music do people hear in your country?"

"Not all of us hear the same music. National rock, tango, folk music, melodic music."

"And which one do you prefer?"

"As I am from a provincial town, I love folk songs."

"Let's hear it. Sing something for us."

"Alyssa." Protested amused the father. At that time Helen and Shaletha came from the kitchen with food and invited everybody to the dining room.

"Well, they saved you..." Said Alyssa. "...for now. But I will make you sing for my friends and me."

"That sounds like a threat..." Said Shaletha smiling." "...and she is capable of fulfilling it."

At the beginning of dinner Ezra offered Adrian to say a prayer.

"Dad, do not embarrass him." Expressed Shaletha. "You do it as usual."

The dinner was quite silent. At the end of the course the conversation returned to the table.

"Mr. Bianchi, what is your religion?

Actually it was the first sentence Helen uttered. It took everyone by surprise by the subject and the opportunity. A moment of silence followed the question.

"But woman! Your daughter's friend comes home for the first time and all you think is asking him about his religion." The husband's tone was scolding.

"No Problem Ezra. I can answer it. I consider myself a Christian."

"You probably have some particular denomination." Insisted the mother, showing the importance the issue had for her.

"I was baptized by the Catholic Church, but as I said before I consider myself just a Christian." The firm tone of the response showed that behind it there was a steadfast conviction. Shaletha raised an eyebrow when she realized that her boyfriend had some core beliefs behind his flexible and easygoing personality she was not aware of.

"Well, all Christians share the essential tenets." Said amicably Ezra with the obvious intention to change the subject.

The conversation went on for a long while jumping form one issue to another. Finally while Helen and Ezra went to the kitchen with the dishes, Shaletha told Adrian.

"We have a long journey and we will have to walk in the dark several blocks. I think it would be convenient to leave now."

They said goodbye to Ezra and Adrian took Helen´s hand and kissed her. Alyssa accompanied them to the door.

"I want you to promise to meet my friends and me at a musical meeting." She told the young man.

" Don´t even dream that I'm going to loan him." Replied Shaletha.

"Why did you react to Alyssa´s proposal that way? Adrian asked as they were walking alone.

"I won´t leave you alone at a meeting with so many young excited vaginas. I already know you like black women."

Now it was the man´s turn laughing.

"How little you trust me!"

" I know these girls. And you tell me, where did that kiss so baroque in my mother´s hand came from?

"Really not even I know. I already told you that in my country women get friendly kissed."

"I think you left her pretty perplex... Well, it was a good meeting, I'm relieved."

CHAPTER 9

"HE PROBABLY IS AN ATHEIST, or at least an agnostic".

"But Helen, you've heard that when you asked he defined himself as a Christian."

"But I've also heard that he left the Catholic Church and now has no denomination. He is certainly not going to church, so he has no guidance or direction."

Ezra was getting angry with his wife.

"Not everyone needs to have external guidance, many simply will rely on their internal compass."

"So goes the world. Drugs, violence, lies, indiscriminate sex."

"Neither your daughter nor her boyfriend fall into these categories. What you say is totally unfair. I do not know what part of my assertion that this boy helped save your son you did not understand."

At that moment the front door opened and a conversation was heard in the lobby.

"It's Alyssa. It seems she ´s coming with someone."

The girl appeared indeed at the door, accompanied by a very tall young man.

"Oh no! Not in this moment." Ezra whispered to himself.

" Mom, Dad, Let me introduce Ivan Stasevich."

"Hello Ivan." Ezra stretched his hand forward. "I am Ezra Moore and this is my wife Helen."

Helen was obviously going through a very bitter trance and looked down to the floor with a contained grimace. Alyssa was puzzled and Ivan managed to say.

"If this is a bad time, I ..."

"Not at all. Helen does not feel quite well but please come to the living room. Alyssa lead your friend. And I'll join you right away."

Ezra turned to his wife with a serious look and snapped.

"I'll never forgive you if you make such a snub to your daughter. You understand me. There is a minimum hospitality we give to all visitors. If you want, go to your room, I'll give some excuse for your absence."

The man walked resolutely to the living room and asked her daughter.

"Alyssa, have you asked your friend if he wants something to drink?"

"Not yet Dad."

"Where are your manners? Bring us some coffee please."

The conversation went on quickly since all three were sociable people.

"Is Ivan a common name in Russia?"

"Yes, Mr. Moore, it is about as common as John is here."

"Where do you live?"

"With my parents in Brighton Beach near Coney Island, but during my studies at the University I rented a small apartment in Manhattan, along with two other classmates."

"Where were you born?"

"In the outskirts of Moscow. My parents came to the States when I was one year old ."

"What do you study?"

"Mechanical engineering."

"And you're a good student?"

At that point Alyssa interjected.

"Ivan and I know each other from high school. He was the best student in our class, he's very intelligent."

As any parent Ezra would have continued his practical examination in order to determine what kind of boy his daughter was having an affair with, but then Helen appeared. She looked haggard and crestfallen and sat with the others in silence.

"Mom, Ivan was telling us to what church he belongs. Right Ivan?"

"Huh! ... Yes, yes. In my family we are Orthodox Christians."

" And do you attend your church?" Asked Helen. The girl stared at Ivan.

"Yes." He replied in a confident tone."My mother took me to church when I was a kid together with my brothers and I acquired the habit."

"Merciful God." Ezra muttered as he felt the lump that had formed in his stomach was unleashing.

After the meeting Ezra accompanied the youth, who had announced that they would go out together.

" Alyssa, at what time are you coming back?"

" Before midnight, Dad."

"I'll bring her Mr. Moore. Don 't worry." Added Ivan.

As the three of them went out Ezra saw that all the neighbors were watching their activities. The next minute the Moore would be the center of the neighborhood gossip. His heart gave a new turn as he saw Alyssa and Ivan climbing a powerful Japanese motorcycle that was parked on the sidewalk.

"Hey! Ivan." Added unexpectedly Ezra. "If you sell that bike I think with the money you can buy a small car."

"What? Ah, yes, yes. Surely."

Ezra wondered what the reason for his daughter 's funny face was.

He had gone to visit Shaletha at a time when he knew she would be alone. Of all his relatives he had the best understanding with his eldest daughter and he knew he could entrust her all his concerns as a parent.

" ... The problem is that your mother takes all the sermons of Reverend Lewis too literally.

"Dad, you are also a member of that congregation. Why do not you go talk to the Pastor?"

"You cannot expect that he will change his preaching at my requests."

" No, but he can talk to Mom and clarify some concepts. Lewis is not a troglodyte. He has always advised you well and realistically."

"It's an idea. I'll see what ..."

At that time Adrian arrived at the apartment. Ezra mentally noted that the boy, despite having his own rented house in Queens, was spending practically every day at his daughter´s home.

"How are you Adrian? Well, just I was already leaving."

"No way Dad. You will have dinner with us."

The Reverend Lewis was an imposing black man both in his Sunday church apparel as his everyday street clothes.

"Ezra. How are you? I haven´t seen you for a long time in worship."

The meeting had a brief introduction time, but Lewis quickly guessed that some special purpose was bringing Ezra Moore to his church, so he urged him to elaborate.

" ... You say that Helen has reacted badly against your daughters´ friends. Religion has nothing to do with reversed racism. On Sunday I will ask her to stay with me after the service and talk about this issue. And tell me, what you know of Zion?"

Ezra opened his heart and told the pastor what he knew about his son from the moment he left him in Albany; news was really sparse. The clergyman thought for a moment.

" Do you remember Thomas Williams, the policeman ?"

"Of course. We went to high school together. I think he must be retired by now".

"He is not. I think he will retire soon but at present he is still in the NYPD. Now he is a lieutenant and the second in charge of the local precinct. He is also a member of my congregation." Lewis made a moment of silence." The murder case in which Zion was involved happened in his precinct."

Ezra looked at him intently.

"What are you trying to tell me?"

"That you should go and talk to Thomas."

"MR. MOORE, LT. WILLIAMS will receive you now."

Ezra entered his old friend's austere office. Both men embraced for a while.

"How long since we last met, Ezra?"

"I reckon that about twenty years. No less than fifteen anyway."

After some exchanges of information about mutual friends, Williams decided to cut to the chase and said.

"I know why you are here. The Reverend Lewis told me of your visit in advance and asked me to help you, but actually I was waiting you before he did."

"How is that?"

"It's in relation to the shooting of a week ago. Those who died were Leroy White, a friend of your son and two thugs of a gang that owns much of the drug trade in Harlem, one of the dead being a man of some importance in that gang. When looking at Leroy's friends immediately arose Zion's name and as he disappeared from the streets where usually our people find him, we were quick to make the math. Our current hypothesis is that the gang had ordered Zion and Leroy's murders because they were trying to displace them from some major drug distribution points, and your son somehow managed to escape. Do not answer me if you don't want to."

" Thomas, Zion fired only in self-defense and it is a miracle that he has come out alive because he is not a man of action and a shooter."

"Well, say no more in order not to incriminate yourself. Hey, I imagine that are in contact with your brother who was a cop in Chicago ..."

"Gary, Indiana, near Chicago. His name is Jacob."

" ... Well, I guess you've resorted to him to ... let´s say...advise you about your child. Tell Jacob to call me home." Williams wrote a phone number on a piece of paper. "Let us have a talk among professionals."

Ezra thanked him and was about to withdraw when an idea popped into his head.

"May I ask you another favor? Could you find out something for me about some people in Brighton Beach?"

" I hope you are dealing with the Russian mafia?"

"I really do not know. My youngest daughter is in love with the son of a merchant of that neighborhood. I wonder who these people are."

I have to contact with our colleagues in Coney Island. Who are they?"

"The father is a certain Yuri Stasevich, and Alyssa´s friend is called Ivan."

" Is it trouble for you saying the word boyfriend? Believe me, I understand, I'm going through the same process. About your request, give a few days to investigate."

"How can I thank you for your help?"

"In due time we will tell your son to turn himself in. I want him to do it with me. Do you always live in the same house?"

"Yes."

"When Jacob advises you that the time has come, you make sure Zion is in your home. I'll go look for him myself."

CHAPTER 10

THE NEXT DAY EZRA MOORE received a call from his brother Jacob.

"How is Zion?"

"Badly but improving. We have enrolled him under a phony name in a detoxification program. It is a long term process."

"And he agreed to go?"

"Yes. What is already in itself is a progress. Hey! Guess who called me."

"Surely Tho ..."

"Shh. No unnecessary names. We were discussing the best strategy for your child."

"I'm listening."

"In an eventual trial for the alleged murder of the thugs he has the upper hand. Possibly they will condemn him for evading justice or the like but he can certainly claim self-defense. There will be a short sentence, whether bailable or not. But he will be able to put an end to the issue and turn back to his life. I hear you moaning. You old fool. Are you crying?"

"Go ahead."

"The issue to decide is the right time to turn him in. If he does it now he will be called as a witness against the rival gang, exposing himself and exposing you as his family to threats and retaliation. He might have to be enrolled in a witness protection program and hide for the rest of his life."

"I understand, it would be a nightmare for him and for us. Is there any other possibility?"

"Yes. Your former high school classmate ...shh, no names...confided me that they are very close to condemn this gang without relying on your child´s testimony . His subsequent trial would be independent and not so exposed to reprisals. I recommend following this course of action. I need your approval because Zion is not yet able to decide for himself with clarity on such an important issue."

"You have my consent, of course."

"Don´t you need to consult first with Helen?"

"I´d rather not! Regarding Zion his mother until now has been part of the problem. I take full responsibility by myself."

Two days later, Ezra received another call, this time from Thomas Williams.

"Ezra, I obtained data on the people of Brighton Beach you had asked me."

"I´m listening."

"So far there is no information connecting Yuri Stasevich or members of his family directly with violent criminal acts of the Russian mafia or other sources."

"But...?"

"Well, this Stasevich is a powerful merchant and he could be somehow washing black money. I do not know if you want that for Alyssa."

"No doubt I don´t. The boy Ivan is a student and he is not living in Brighton Beach right now. Sure he is not personally involved in the possible dirty activities of his family."

"What will you do?"

"You also have two daughters. What wouldn´t you do to keep the girls happy. I'll think of something and I'll let you know."

"Yes, I assure you it is easy for me to put myself in your shoes, but our problems are different. Let me know if you need anything else from me."

"Another thing. I have just approved the plan outlined by you and Jacob for Zion. I appreciate your participation in this issue too."

Just when Ezra ended the communication with Williams Helen entered the room. Ezra told himself.

"We will face all the problems at once. I'll put all the meat on the grill. "

"Helen, I want to talk to you."

The voluntary parish clerk entered Reverend Lewis´ narrow office.

"Helen Moore wants to talk to you. She had made an appointment."

"Yes, yes. I remember. Let her in."

Helen entered the office somewhat crestfallen. Lewis was quick to realize it. He already knew the issue and had prepared some thoughtful responses.

Helen described the family situation with the sincerity with which she usually spoke in her scarce pastoral visits.

" ... And suddenly ... my two daughters have been dating men from outside the community. I feel that we are working to dissolve the black family in our country."

The woman continued expressing her fears and feelings, whilst the pastor reflected what specific advice would be really useful and opportune for the troubled woman. His twenty year relationship with her and her family would guide him as he began speaking. When he judged that Helen had already fully expressed her fears Lewis decided to address the issue without euphemisms.

"Helen, you're right that the preservation of the black family has always been the goal of our congregation and it still is. But times change. When we expressed our desires in those words there was no chance that our kids could find happiness with partners from other races, and if any white man ever approached a black woman was only for a fleeting relationship and finally return to his own circle leaving her broken-hearted."

Helen nodded as she heard once again the familiar reasoning. Lewis paused to emphasize his following words.

"Well, Helen, that situation has changed radically in the recent years. Our church has been following the evolution of demographic trends in our country and in the world at large." Lewis paused again to give a proper cadence to his words. Then he continued.

"Statistics in our country show that marriages between black women and white men are the fastest growing group among interracial relationships and are no longer just isolated incidents but a definite trend."

Helen did not expect to hear the pastor say those words and moved uneasy in her chair. Lewis perceived and interpreted the gesture, but decided to go ahead.

"Not only that. The same statistics show that the divorce rate among these couples is less than half the rate of the divorces in marriages between white partners and one quarter of divorces between black men and white women. Do you understand what those numbers mean?"

Helen looked at him quizzically. Lewis went on.

"It means that this trend opens new doors for our youth, that those doors can lead to happiness rather than sorrow and that we must change our prejudices if we don't want to be left out of the real story with real people and raise unnecessary conflicts to our young."

"What is important then?" Asked the distraught woman.

"That we must change some terms of our goal. Instead of talking about the protection of the black family we have to talk about the protection of the Christian family in general."

After the meeting with Lewis, Helen decided to walk home instead of taking the subway. She wanted to process what she had heard and that had hit her like a speeding train. As she walked down the familiar streets Helen felt that a knot in her stomach started unleashing and that a dim light inside her took on an unexpected shine. Perhaps after all she could fulfill her role as a mother without antagonizing the wishes of her daughters.

CHAPTER 11

EZRA HAD BEEN MEDITATING about the best way to approach Ivan´s father. His goal was clear but how to address it was a different story. He would ask an appointment to such Yuri and then ... then what?

"Stasevich is Russian and I am American; he's white and I´m black; he is Orthodox if he really has a religion and I´m Baptist; he has probably had a senior position in the former Soviet Union and I have fought against communism. Do we have something in common to use it as an anchor and reference point? ... Of course, we are both traders. I´ll talk to him as a merchant."

At the time Alyssa and Ivan entered the living room and Ezra stood up and approached them. After greeting he addressed straight to the boy.

"Ivan, I need your father's phone number."

The young man, somewhat surprised cleared his throat and said.

"Of course Mr. Moore. I´ll send it in a what's app message."

Alyssa looked somewhat upset and started saying.

"But Dad what ..."

At that time Helen entered the house increasing Ezra´s distress by the presence of the young Russian.

Helen lifted her head and said with an unexpected smile.

"Hello everyone. Ivan, how are you?"

After that she walked upstairs to her rooms leaving everyone perplexed.

"Mr. Moore, Mr. Stasevich will receive you in a few minutes. He is ending a conference call." Said the secretary with a strong Slavic accent. "May I offer coffee?"

"No thanks. I'm fine."

Ezra took a magazine written in Russian that was on the table in front of him, but almost immediately the office door opened and a tall, burly man about fifty-five years old emerged. The blond hair was partially graying and Ezra noticed he had a strong resemblance to his son, or rather the reverse.

"Mr. Moore. Come in please."

After a formal and inconsequential presentation Stasevich said bluntly.

"I guess the issue that brings you here today is the relationship between our children. Let me ask if you oppose to it, because in that case you should not be talking to me."

Ezra was not discouraged by the Russian straightforward style; actually he preferred to enter the potentially conflictive topic as soon as possible.

"No, I am not opposed to it at all. I would have no reasons."

"Is it your wife who is then opposed?"

A cold sweat ran down Ezra´s back. Actually at that time, given the recent events, he did not even know the answer. There was no doubt that the Russian had some previous information so that there was no point in playing hide and seek.

"That has been overcome. Neither is that. My daughter is a very pretty and intelligent girl as evidenced by her studies but she is not very skilled in human affairs so the way I understand my role as a father leads me to find out about her relationships."

The Russian nodded and replied smiling.

"I've fleetingly seen her and she is really beautiful. Ivan is also a very attractive and highly intelligent boy, no doubt traits inherited from his mother who is a mathematician. His grades in high school and in college, as you probably already know, are among the best in his class."

Ezra felt reassured, his commercial strategy was working effectively. It was a two businessmen talk in a kind of barter, where each one highlighted the benefits of his product. He did not even dare to think what would happen if Helen found out about that conversation.

" ... And Ivan is a very coveted candidate among Russian women in our community, not only in Brighton Beach."

" ... Alyssa can choose boys of any ethnicity. At high school all black and white young boys were after her ..."

At a certain point the secretary came into the office with coffees, served them and walked out.

"Mr. Moore. What is really worrying you?" Asked the Russian, using the break to get down to business.

Ezra answered truthfully and candidly. He feared that her daughter could get entangled in unclear economic activities. He expected that having expressed his feelings so crudely would not offend the Russian and abort the negotiations. Stasevich thought for a while and finally answered.

"I understand your concerns. I'm going to tell you something confidential. Last year I trusted my oldest son an absolutely legitimate business newly established in San Francisco, and am planning to let Ivan run a small ranch I'm buying right now in Montana, also a totally legitimate venture. Our business in Brighton Beach is absolutely legal, but I think at some point our young people should seek fresh air."

The conversation lasted for another half hour but Ezra had already achieved his purpose. His only regret was that he could not share what he had just learned with Shaletha. However...on a second thought. He knew he could count on Shaletha´s discretion.

Ezra was already retiring when they heard the sound of keys in the apartment door; they assumed that Adrian was likely returning from his job. Unexpectedly Shaletha planted a kiss on her father´s forehead.

"What did I do right to deserve that?"

"It's for all you have done for your children! This is my father who was lost and now is back."

"That sounds a bit biblical, doesn't it?"

"It's the way I feel about what you are doing."

Ezra greeted Adrian and left. As her boyfriend entered the apartment Shaletha said.

"Before I forget, Arionna invited us to dinner on Friday at her home."

The news pleased the young man. Shaletha and he had little social life and Arionna and Kevin were the only two people who were close friends.

"We haven't met since Arionna communicated her pregnancy. Shouldn't we invite them at least once?"

"Okay, let's think about a date in the coming days. Come, I want to discuss an issue with you."

They sat in the in the living room couches.

"I want you to move to this apartment with me." Said Shaletha with no preamble. " It does not make sense to pay two rents and double all the other expenses. The last time you were at your apartment was more than a week ago. Our relationship is already known and accepted by all who care about us and by my neighbors."

"So you are asking me to move only for financial and social reasons." Replied Adrian with mock anger.

Shaletha sat on his legs letting her skirt roll aside and showing off their legs.

" Exactly, just for that.".

"Okay. I will consider it." Answered the man introducing his right hand between her thighs. "You'll have to do something to convince me."

"Let me think what I can do."

Arionna served tea. Her pregnancy was noticeable and now she moved more cautiously. Shaletha spoke with a certain pride of all her father's adventures to meet the needs of his children, all of very different nature. At her friend's request she was doing a description of Ivan. Shaletha was telling the studies of the young man, but Arionna shook her head.

"All that does not interest me. You say he's tall and handsome. What color are his eyes?"

"Well, I did not really noticed that."

"Moonshine. You say that in order not to arouse Adrian's jealousy" Then she turned to Adrian and told him.

"You need to know that there are three things a woman always looks at: the man's eyes on one side and the hairstyle and shoes of the other women on the other. The shoes have priority."

Kevin laughed at his wife's colorful description. She then turned back to Adrian and asked.

"And what do men first look at in a woman? What do you watch yourself?"

The young man shifted a little uncomfortably in his chair.

"I? Eh, well, I do not know ... maybe her eyes or her smile."

"That's Moonshine too!" Roared Shaletha."When I first met him in the cafeteria I watched him by the mirror and caught him staring at my behind."

New laugh Kevin, who added.

"That probably comes from his Italian genes. They are known for that preference."

"No one can criticize him for looking your ass." Completed Arionna. " It rarely goes unnoticed."

" Now that I think about it. Who knows how my story would have been without it?"

"Without your ass? There would be no story." Replied Arionna whilst her husband burst into laughter.

"Without that mirror. I'm serious."

The rhetorical question remained unanswered.

"By the way, let me tell you that Adrian will come to live in my apartment, so we'll have him in Brooklyn Heights on a permanent basis."

"That is wonderful news; I'm glad for you. You can finally have him all the time."

"Arionna, you make it sound a bit possessive. Adrian already spends most of the time at home and very little in his own apartment. The change is not so big."

"Pretexts. Of course you have to be possessive about your man. Listen, we have been talking with Kevin to invite you both at home again. Why not once he has moved?"

"He has planned it for Saturday morning."

"Then we invite them to dinner that same day."

The women were preparing food in the kitchen and Kevin and Adrian were in the living room with a glass of whiskey each. The homeowner had made a fortuitous observation while the boy was staring with a lost look and leaving a question unanswered.

"What do you think about it?" Kevin reiterated his question. His interlocutor had a slight shock as he reconnected with reality.

"Excuse me, Kevin. I did not hear what you said. Can you please repeat it?"

Instead of doing what the boy asked Kevin thought for a moment. Finally his face showed that he had made a decision. His long experience as a teacher leading a classroom told him that the young man, usually attentive and prompt in his responses, had something that was worrying him; as had also observed the normal talks between Shaletha and Adrian he sensed that it was not a couple problem so he dared to face it.

"Adrian, I realize there is a problem that is eating you away and I think I'm the closest thing to a friend that you have in this country. If you need and want to share the problem with someone this is the time and I am the person."

The boy stared at him, as if he was also processing a decision. He took a long sip of his whiskey, no doubt to encourage him and began his story.

"You know I'm an illegal immigrant, since my visa has expired six months ago and therefore I am working in a precarious way." Adrian made a break and took another sip of whiskey.

"The people I work for are under pressure to legalize all their personnel and my boss, who is also my friend, warned me that they cannot keep me on the payroll anymore."

"Unless you regularize your situation?"

"Yes."

The conversation, led by Kevin's questions delved on the case details. Finally he asked.

"Have you talked to Shaletha about this?"

"Not yet. I know what she is going to say."

"What do you think she's going to say?"

"That I must not worry about that, because she earns enough to keep us both. But as you'll understand that it is a situation that I am not willing to accept. I'm not a gigolo or a parasite."

"Well." Mused Kevin." Do not talk to her yet. As you know Arionna is a lawyer, and among other things she constantly deals with such situations. She has helped many people before and will certainly help you, since you're her best friend's fiancé."

Kevin got up and refilled their glasses.

"I'll be calling you to come home alone and meet us in a couple of days. I repeat that you should not discuss this with Shaletha yet. She is a sensitive person and will suffer if you do not have a solution in sight."

Arionna sat in front of Adrian while her husband watched the scene. The usually festive countenance of the woman had become a professional face.

"Adrian, I will ask you a series of questions and I need you to answer them accurately, because the details are important."

"I understand."

"Did you bring your passport?"

The boy handed it in silence; a certain tension could be perceived in his general attitude. Arionna toured the pages also in silence. Finally she said.

'"The first good news is that you have entered the country legally, that is to say an immigration officer has stamped you passport when entering at the JF Kennedy Airport. If you had entered inside the trunk of a car or in any other unlawful manner the issue would be more complicated."

The woman looked at her husband and then at Adrian´s eyes. She said to him.

"You've got the solution to your fingertips."

"What do you mean?"

"You can regularize your situation and get your green card for permanent residency by marrying an American citizen."

Kevin was looking intently at the young man face to see his reaction. What he observed was a loosening of certain facial muscles in a clear sign of relief. He asked sarcastically."

"Do you know any woman who would make the sacrifice to marry you?"

Adrian looked puzzled for a moment but then smiled and answered.

"I do not know. I have to go out and ask around."

"For the whole process you need an attorney." Added Arionna with a mock hostile gesture. "You do that and I will seek to get the death penalty for both of you." After watching her husband she said." You as the instigator and mastermind of the crime. So get ready for the needle."

"Please let´s get serious again." Adrian said in a pleading tone.

"Then I draw the conclusion that you're willing to get married."Arionna insisted.

"Yes, Yes."

"With Shaletha?"

"Of course. Who else?"

"Now you must formally ask her if she wants to marry you." Said the woman "... no, do not take it for granted. I'll talk to Shaletha and convince her to put some conditions. It is her opportunity to fully squeeze you."

"More than she does?" Asked plaintively the young man.

"You can always squeeze a lemon a little further."

Kevin turned serious and asked his wife.

"Why don't you tell us how the procedure would be?"

"Adrian has exceeded the term of his visa, but that can be solved by a process that I have carried out many times. You can file both forms simultaneously, that is the marriage and the residency applications. I see you have not left the United States territory since you came."

"That's right."

"It's essential that you do not leave the US until you have all your papers in order, otherwise you cannot re-enter. You have to be represented by a lawyer throughout the process."

"Do you know any good one?" Asked ironically Kevin

"We must argue, that is Shaletha must allege, that your departure if you are forced to leave the country would cause her pain and difficulties."

The conversation then led to issues related with forms to fill and legal procedures. At nine p.m. Adrian said goodbye with a more or less elaborate plan. He hurried to Shaletha's home, about three blocks distant.

Upon opening the door the woman, somewhat altered scolded him.

"Where are you coming from? It is very late and I did not know what to think. Couldn´t you have called me earlier?"

In answer to the flood of questions Adrian raised rose her from the floor and asked.

"Would you marry me?"

CHAPTER 12

THE FLIGHT FROM BUENOS Aires arrived fifteen minutes early. Adrian felt his stomach shrank by the stress. At his side Shaletha's was looking at his face, aware of her boyfriend's emotional state. Passengers that had checked in baggage began to emerge from the sliding doors. The boy pressed her hand to relieve some of his anxiety. He finally exclaimed.

"There they are! They are behind the Chinese family". When travelers arrived to the spacious lobby Adrian released the hand he was squeezing and ran to the newcomers. Shaletha was moved observing the unexpected scene. The four were embraced in a long hug with no words. The tall man's eyes looked humid even at a distance while the mother clutched her son with her eyes filled with tears. The red haired boy next to them had also his face altered by emotion. Certainly none of the four was prepared and they were overwhelmed by intense feelings. What impressed Shaletha was seeing the usually impassive Adrian weeping uncontrollably as he reunited with his family again. According to the calculations of the woman, the young man had not seen his folks for a couple of years, including the time he had spent in Rio de Janeiro. Finally the tall man made a interrogative gesture toward Shaletha undoubtedly wondering if it was her who their son had to introduce. Adrian took her mother's bag and approached his girlfriend. Shaletha could not escape the emotion of the moment and felt her eyes also moist.

"My fiancée Shaletha. These are my parents Sebastian and Teresa, and he is my younger brother Federico."

Teresa rose slightly to kiss Shaletha on the cheek, which did not take her by surprise as she was already aware of the customs of her boyfriend compatriots.

Sebastian extended his hand and introduced in very formally in Spanish.

"Sebastian Bianchi. Nice to meet you."

Federico did not know which of his parents to imitate so that Shaletha took the initiative and also kissed his cheek.

"What a good looking gentleman! How old are you?"

"Fourteen." Answered in English the boy.

Most of the conversation until they reached the airport parking lot was in Spanish, and dealt with issues related to the trip. Shaletha watched in silence, absorbing perceptions and feelings. Sebastian Bianchi was a tall, slender man, and no doubt his son had inherited his general physical appearance and eyes color; his skin was tanned by the sun and the elements and evidenced a life spent outdoors; his manners were restrained and his conversation brief. Shaletha thought everything in him revealed a farmer, from Argentina, the United States or elsewhere.

Teresa was shorter, sturdier and her hair was reddish, a trait her children inherited. Certainly she talked constantly inquiring information on her son's life. Finally she made a comment expecting Adrian to translate it into English.

"My mother is telling you that I also have a sister, named Beatriz, who could not come because she is married and has three children, one of them one year old and two schoolchildren."

While Shaletha looked on and listened the chat between the components of the family, although she did not understand almost anything of the conversations she was invaded by a sense of tenderness and pride for what would soon become her family. She had never had such feelings for white people and realized that some still existing barriers within her she was not aware of began to dissolve. So far her relationship was personal and sentimental with Adrian, with whom she was bound by love but now the veil of the reality that was behind her man including his family was being lifted. Suddenly Shaletha came back to reality as she heard Adrian was talking to her.

"Sorry. What did you say?"

"My mother congratulated me for having found such a beautiful woman."

It was not the first praise Shaletha received; she actually received them all the time. But this one seemed especially significant and auspicious.

Adrian had made reservations for his family in a hotel in Brooklyn Heights, near Shaletha´s apartment. The proximity was important because the Bianchi spoke little English and were unaccustomed to leave their farm, their town and their country.

At night Shaletha hosted a dinner at her apartment and invited not only to Adrian´s parents but also Arionna and Kevin. The latter spoke Spanish learned in his childhood and practiced on a sabbatical year he had spent years before in Costa Rica.

"I did not think I would remember it so well. I haven´t used it years." Confessed satisfied Kevin after a while." Languages return to your head when you need them."

This removed from Adrian´s shoulders the burden of being the only translator of all that was spoken at the meeting.

The talk with Sebastian Bianchi led naturally to his status as a farmer.

"How big is your farm?"Asked Kevin.

"Four hundred hectares that is about a thousand acres."

"Good farming lands?"

"In Hughes, Province of Santa Fe."

"It's in the heart of the so called *wet pampas*" Explained Adrian. "Something equivalent to the corn belt in the United States."

"That is, some of the best agricultural land in the world."

Sebastian proudly continued answering Kevin's questions about the methods and techniques used on his farm. Finally the latter said.

"I see you are very updated. No-Tillage is recommended to avoid erosion and maintain fields' productivity and the same can be said of the practice of crop rotation methods."

"And how come you know all that?" Asked Arionna.

"'Do not forget that my doctoral thesis was about the impact of agricultural techniques in the development of civilizations. Since then I kept myself fairly updated, though obviously more in what refers to the historical aspect rather than the technical."

The conversation then turned to Federico's studies.

"I attend an agricultural technical school in a nearby town." Explained the boy.

After an hour of talk Arionna, whose fifth month pregnancy was already perceptible said.

"If you do not mind I would like to leave. I had a day of hard work and I'm almost exhausted."

"All right." Answered Shaletha. But I invite you for this coming Saturday. We're going to visit my parents in Harlem and I would like you joined us."

"Fair enough." Exclaimed Arionna with her usual critical tone. "It seems that we will finally get to know our best friend's parents. Although Harlem is just a few subway stations from here we'll meet them at the same time than Adrian's parents who come from thousands of miles."

"*Touché.*" Replied Shaletha

"In Spanish we say "better late than never" " Added Adrian who had just joined the conversation.

The five people traveled a little tight in the old Toyota loaned by Adrian's friend and driven by him. The Bianchi folks looked absorbed the colorful spectacle of Harlem at that time. At one point the driver announced.

"We have arrived. That's the house. You please get down here and Shaletha will guide you. Meanwhile I'll try to find a place to park. Arionna and Kevin will arrive at any time."

Shaletha could barely contain the urge to see how the meeting between her family and her future in-laws developed. The natural tension expected in every woman at a meeting of that nature was increased by the fact that both families belonged to different universes, separated by thousands of miles, different languages, different ethnic backgrounds, cultural patterns as far away as there could be between city dwellers of a black New York neighborhood and inhabitants of a small rural town in Argentina. Even religious beliefs diverged, as the Moore family was a stronghold of the Baptist church in their quarter while Adrian had anticipated that his family consisted of agnostics since the arrival of his socialist grandfather from northern Italy. This issue itself could be a source of conflict so Shaletha had asked her father to avoid it relying on his usual discretion and intuitive wisdom.

The Moore had prepared the house to welcome their guests in a dignified manner, and the Argentineans were wearing against Adrian's advice the clothes they had brought for the wedding ceremony.

Shaletha began making introductions trying to overcome language barriers as the door bell rang again and Arionna, whose belly was growing daily, appeared accompanied Kevin, who took charge of the translations, although they themselves have never met the homeowners until then.

When Adrian arrived, after finally having parked the car four blocks from the house they were all already sitting around cups of coffee and therefore he missed the impact of the first moment of encounter. From the lobby the young man could see that the atmosphere was relaxed and peaceful, which made him heave a sigh of relief.

For a long time the talk focused on Shaletha and Adrian's childhood and adolescence, fueled by the interest of both mothers who had left Kevin the role of interpreter under the watchful presence of Arionna; the woman had self-imposed role of circumventing any potential conflict trait. Ezra invited the men to see his collection of ancient coins of which he was very proud. As Adrian was not aware of the numismatic hobby of his future father-in-law this evidenced how much he ignored of his future family. For that reason he decided to return to the meeting between his mother and Helen where he could learn many details of Shaletha´s life he did not know.

In a moment, a clamor was heard at the door, Adrian guessed that the noise heralded the arrival of Alyssa, Shaletha´s younger sister. Indeed the girl appeared surrounded by several girls of about the same age, doubtless neighborhood friends and school. As soon as they entered the room the girls´ eyes fell upon Federico, who had hitherto been silent in an isolated corner of the house, oblivious to the different chats. Alyssa nodded to her sister in a rather obvious way requesting her to introduce the boy. As a result Federico joined the youth group and soon all of them left the house. Teresa Bianchi´s apprehensive eyes followed him with through a window facing the street until her husband asked her.

"What is the matter, woman?"

"It's Federico. Look at him!" As she said this Teresa pointed at his son´s head, a red dot among all the girls around him. " He is only fourteen."

"So what? The girls around him are also young."

"But they are city girls, very roguish. Federico has barely left Hughes in his life."

"Good chance for him to open his eyes. What has been good for Adrian will not be bad for Federico."

Teresa shook her head as if to scare off all the ideas that came to her mind. Arionna suddenly emerged from nowhere, took her by the arm and began to tell her very slowly things in English that Teresa could only partially understand but had the virtue of calming her mind.

Understanding the situation and the purpose of the action, the Argentine woman gave her one of her frank smiles.

"So it's you from whom Adrian inherited his seductive smiles." Said Arionna in the hope that the other woman would understand. "I guess he has broken hearts back there in your town."

CHAPTER 13

THE WEDDING PREPARATIONS had been extremely stressing and were on the verge of shipwreck more than once. This was at least Shaletha's perception, since she had taken the matter in her hands. Indeed, the insinuations of some of her friends to leave everything in the hands of wedding organizers had received her resounding answer.

"They charge a fortune for whatever little they do, and ultimately I would have to take all decisions anyway, especially with my personality and my profession. No! I have better uses for the money."

Those who knew her had no choice but to recognize the wisdom of those words. However Shaletha regretted more than once of her decision.

One of the tasks Shaletha delegated was the selection of the church in which the ceremony was to be performed; this issue was handed over to Arionna who already had her ideas. The woman was a member of a Presbyterian Church in Brooklyn Heights, which defined itself as an "inclusive and diverse Christian community", which according Arionna responded perfectly to the characteristics of the couple. Kevin, who was actually attached to the parish through the music festivals rather than theology shared his wife's preferences.

Shaletha kept all preparations secret, to the relief of Adrian, who never showed too interested in them. In the previous days the young man concentrated in touring the city with his parents and brother and even traveled a full weekend to Washington DC on a rental car.

The day of the ceremony the bride finally came together with her godparents and met Adrian and his family at the door of the church.

The woman looked resplendent in a long and simple wedding dress. The Afro hairstyle hair exhibited an entirely different look Adrian was used to. The contrast between the white dress and her brown skin was simply dazzling. A magnificent necklace around her throat enhanced the outfit with the issuance of a thousand flashes as it reflected light. The young man stood momentarily with his mouth open and without control of his acts. His father lightly touched his arm to make him react and he could just hear his mother cry.

"OMG! She is truly beautiful."

Shaletha understood enough and the expression made her blush as usual.

Sebastian and Adrian Bianchi had rented tuxedos for the ceremony and it was clear that they were not comfortable in their outfits, especially the first. Teresa and Federico were soberly dressed and looked a bit too formal.

The whole Moore family was in the church as well as many of their lifetime neighbors and several Adrian colleagues. At one point Shaletha saw a man dressed in a hooded garment approach her in a somewhat furtive attitude, and great was her emotion as she recognized her brother Zion, who had returned to New York taking risks for his life. The two siblings merged in a heartfelt and speechless hug full of tears.

"How come you are here?" Said Shaletha sobbing.

"I could not miss it, sister, for no reason in the world."

Ezra came up and hugged his children. He told Shaletha.

" This was our surprise. Zion will be present only in the religious ceremony. He cannot go back to Harlem for reasons you will understand."

"And will he ever go back home and to our neighborhood?"

"Eventually but not yet."

By the time that Shaletha was about to enter the temple Arionna stood before her and said.

"Wait, I know you have something new because your dress is. Are you wearing something old?"

"Yes, this necklace belonged to my grandmother and my mother just gave it to me."

"And are you wearing something borrowed and something blue?"

"Not really."

"Take this light blue shawl. Not much at odds with your dress. You will return it to me after the ceremony."

"What are you talking about?" Asked intrigued Adrian.

"About old American traditions ." Replied visibly moved Alyssa. "It is assumed that if the bride wears on the wedding day something new, something old, something borrowed and something blue it will bring luck to the couple in their conjugal life."

"And shouldn't the groom wear something too?" Asked the man.

"The groom is out of the picture here." Answered crudely Arionna. "He is just part of the decoration, only one element without which there would be no wedding."

After the religious ceremony, conducted by a female pastor, attendees went to a ball hall in Harlem Ezra Moore had rented for the party. He had obviously not spared expenses; the site was decorated quite lavishly; the Moore family was well known people in the area and Ezra was to deliver his eldest daughter in an unforgettable way.

Adrian's parents immediately found partners with whom to chat in Spanish among his son's coworkers, mostly people of the Puerto Rican community in New York. Federico again found himself surrounded by girls and out of sight as soon the crowd began to dance; his mother was confined to control that he was not drinking alcohol every time she saw him, which did not happen very often. Adrian received countless jokes of his colleagues by the dazzling beauty of his bride, who was not known by most of them. Alyssa had been accompanied by his Russian friend and had become another focus of interest of the audience.

Through a window a figure covered by a long coat with the hood thrown over his eyes watched the events of the party from the street. A groan came from the chest of Zion Moore finding the price to pay for all his youthful mistakes.

Tired of dancing with her husband and almost all male competitors, Shaletha sat in a chair almost fainting. Beside her sat a Latina woman, one of Adrian's companions, although she immediately clarified that she did not have a close relationship with the groom. The woman, named Rosa, had a drink in her hand that certainly had been preceded by others. Her mood was excellent and alcohol did not inhibit the consistency of her conversation, at least not completely.

"Dear." She told Shaletha."You're as beautiful as a bride can be. And I do not say it as a compliment. You will see by yourself in all the pictures that have been taken. Your wedding dress is splendid."

Shaletha said that she was a fashion designer by profession, and had extensive experience in wedding gowns.

"Well, in that case you must be very good at your job."

The two women hit it off from the start and spent a long time talking. Rosa said she was between two romances and had separated from his last boyfriend the week before.

"I even had once an Argentine boyfriend. It was an affair that lasted nearly a year. One of the longest I have ever had, and for a time I was in love with Gaston.

Rosa told in sparkling form some chapters of her relationship, uninhibited in part by alcohol.

"... You know? They are quite different from other Latinos. Proud and sometimes arrogant but on the other side generous lovers, perhaps by the Italian mix. You must know that no one forgets his country though all the time they protest against it. They carry their country and family in their blood, even though they often make them suffer. If you want to keep him never fight against these things ... but with your face and your ass, I do not think you run any risk." Rosa burst into a contagious laugh. Shaletha recalled the mirror scene at the coffee shop the day she met Adrian; stimulated her curiosity and overcoming some resistance thanks to alcohol she added.

"All men are attracted by women behinds."

"Yes, but ... again these Italian genes." The talk was becoming more dispersed with the successive shots.

"Ah! Listen! Another issue is what they call football ... you know, soccer. They are able to forget their wives for a game. Most are fans of one of two clubs ..."

The night ended with a new round of dances. In his drunken joy Shaletha watched her father's face. She did not remember having ever seen his eyes shining with happiness as that night. Then her gaze turned to her mother; her usually dour and tense gesture had relaxed and she smiled at her interlocutors.

"Well Shaletha. It sure was a good thing you did for yours today."

At one point the bride saw her friend Arionna sitting alone. Given her advanced pregnancy she had not drunk a drop of alcohol. Kevin was performing his usual functions of photographer and his wife had a bored expression. Her eyes were glad to see Shaletha, who however did not speak to her and simply stroked the belly and smiled. The two friends exchanged a series of coded messages in their eyes.

That night Sebastian Bianchi had to take over driving back to Brooklyn Heights, as he and Federico were the only ones in sobriety and the boy had no license.

"I hope my Argentine driving license is valid here."

"But Dad, you're not used to driving in New York."

"This car is a Toyota, like my truck."

"But these streets are not rural roads."

"Every so I drive to Rosario and Buenos Aires."

Adrian resigned to the stubbornness of his father and fell asleep almost immediately. Shaletha had rested her head on his shoulder and got asleep as well. Federico, although he had not drunk alcohol, fell exhausted after a night of dancing and excitement. Only Teresa remained awake with her husband, as she mentally reviewed all the welter of experiences lived since their arrival in New York and particularly in her son´s marriage.

When Sebastian left them in front of their building and parked in the corner, Shaletha and Adrian awoke but were still under the effects of the alcohol. After entering noisily into the apartment, the woman said she was not in a position to take off the complicated dress by herself and asked her husband to help her.

As he undid the hooks of the back Shaletha asked.

"Tell me. Are you a fan of Boca Juniors or River Plate?"

The question about Argentine football teams took Adrian aback, who had never talked about that issue with her, so he assumed that his wife had drunk more than expected.

"Neither. I follow Rosario Central, but I'm not a big fan."

"Rosario Central. What is that?"

"Another Team. But tell me, where did you learn about soccer teams in Argentina?"

"If you ever leave me because of that... whatever Central club I´ll kill you." Her speech did not sound too sober.

"Oh my God. Rosa! I see she has been filling your head. You know that she has had an Argentine boyfriend, who had to leave her by her insatiable sexual appetite. Poor Gaston came every morning at the office completely exhausted. She was slowly consuming him up."

At that moment the man managed to completely unbutton her dress and helped his wife to take it off. Afterwards he hugged her, kissed her on the mouth perceiving her ethyl breath and slid his hands from her waist to the buttocks which he toured at will.

"Take your hands off my ass. I'm not a piece of meat, you know."

"Damn Rosa! What other poison has she placed into your head?"

Adrian lifted his wife and placed her on the bed. If he had a purpose in mind he had to put aside because as when he placed her on bed Shaletha was fast asleep and slightly snoring.

Adrian felt his wife was pinching his arm. Immediately after he vaguely heard her voice coming from some remote region. He had been sleeping for scarcely five minutes, or at least so it seemed to him.

"How? What did you say?"

"I need you to make love to me now."

"You need? Five minutes ago you did not want me to touch you behinds, and now ..."

"This is my wedding night, and it is my right and your obligation."

"I'll fall asleep on top of you."

"I'll keep you awake as long as it takes."

After reaching a deep orgasm, Shaletha pulled the body of her husband away, noticing he had actually fallen asleep immediately; the man had done his job. She had dreamed that that was the night in which she was going to complete the unique feature that she had not yet fulfilled in her life and that her whole being was longing for. She had just done what was necessary to achieve it with the man she had long before chosen for it.

Shaletha smiled in the dark, turned into bed and fell asleep.

EPILOGUE

"BUT HAVE YOU TAKEN the test?"

"Not yet, but I know I'm pregnant."

"Shaletha. You know or you want to know?" insisted Arionna.

"Both. Of course I'm going to take the test today or tomorrow."

"Did you say something to Adrian?"

"No."

"Don´t until you are certain. But do you know if he wants it like you?"

"If I want it so badly he will also want it to keep me happy."

"My best friend happens to be an arrogant and self-centered shrew. Don´t you want to know if he wishes it for himself?"

"What I just told you is exactly what he will tell me. For me Adrian is like an open book."

"Selfish bitch. Well, I'll tell you what your husband will really think of having a child with you. He will wholeheartedly want it."

Shaletha stood up and hugged her friend.

"You know, I did not think that that was so simple and easy to achieve. It's like all the scattered pieces of my life going through different paths get suddenly pulled together. Does it make sense or what I say is pure nonsense and self-centered crap as you say?"

"Of course it makes sense. For years I told you that you were overly tied to your work and your personal life was being wasted."

"And everything changed ..." Shaletha stopped and blushed.

"What changed?"

" ... When through the mirror of a cafeteria I caught a handsome young man looking at my ass."

Both burst into laughter.

"Do you know what it was that made me realize I was assembling the loose parts of my life."

"Seeing yourself in the white wedding dress, or enjoying sex as a married woman."

"No. Looking at the bright eyes of my father at the party, or hear my mother-in law admiring her black daughter and especially ..."

"Especially?"

"Briefly seeing my brother whom I did not expect to see again."

Arionna was deeply moved despite his usual habit of keeping both feet on the ground.

When she opened the door to let Arionna come out of the building Shaletha spotted Adrian's long silhouette on the corner obviously coming from the subway station. Her eyes filled with tears.

"What are you waiting for?" Exclaimed Arionna. "Run to meet him!"

"But."

"Do I have to be pushing you all your life? Run."

As he saw his wife running in slippers down the street towards him the surprised Adrian opened his arms.

From the Author

DEAR READER

I appreciate your interest in reading these few words in which I talk about my work. It is a good habit to try to understand what led an author to write a particular book, because the motivations vary from author to author and from book to book.

As a sign of respect for the reader, in all my books I make a thorough previous investigation of the facts the work refers to, particularly considering that many of them take place in places sometimes very far apart from each other and also in various historical periods; my books often travel indeed through dilated stretches in time and space.

These searches are based on my memory, in the large family library and the huge quarry of facts and data existing in the Internet. In the global network everyone can search but not all find the same ... fortunately, since this results in a huge variability and diversity.

The plot of course comes from the imagination and fantasy. This is critical for me and I confess that I would never write a book that I wouldn´t like to read; my interests as a writer and as a reader coincide to a large degree.

My works often take place in exotic locations and refer sometimes to surprising and even paradoxical facts, but never enter the realm of the fantastic and incredible. Moreover, the most bizarre events are often true.

About the Author

LOUIS ALEXANDRE FORESTIER is the pen name an Argentine novelist uses for certain types of narrative, in general *novellas* of erotic nature and books belonging to the noir genre.

The author has lived in New York for years and now resides in Buenos Aires, his hometown. His style is clear and straightforward, and does not hesitate to tackle thorny issues.

Works by Louis Alexandre Forestier

In English
South of Capricorn
Hot Brooklyn Heights
Cristelle
Valentina-Psychological Romance
Nubia- Magickal Thriller
Passionate Interlude
Nubia- Warrior Princess
Shaletha- Romance in Manhattan

In Spanish
Al Sur de Capricornio
Hot Brooklyn Heights
Cristelle
Valentina
Nubia- Suspenso Mágicko
Interludio Pasional
Nubia-Princesa Guerrera
Shaletha- Romance en Manhattan

Coordinates of the Author

Website: https://louisforestiernarrativa.wordpress.com/
Facebook: http://tinyurl.com/hrq7bsy
Twitter: https://twitter.com/forastero010
MAILTO: louisforestier6@gmail